What Was It about Her?

he asked himself. Maybe instead he ought to be asking
what it was about himself that made him respond to such
a stridently sexy woman.

Did an untamed animal lurk beneath his genteel exterior?
He couldn't believe that. After all, he hadn't even glanced
at any of the other scantily clad waitresses.

It wasn't Audrey's sex appeal that captivated him—she
was too buxom, and her makeup was on too thick. But
maybe he was simply trying to fool himself. Maybe his
ability to bake bread, his willingness to iron his own
shirts was all a pose. Maybe beneath his cultivated veneer
he was just another drooling male animal.

Brandon could make no sense of his feelings for Audrey.
Pure lust, he thought. *Call it like it is.*

Dear Reader:

SILHOUETTE DESIRE is an exciting new line of contemporary romances from Silhouette Books. During the past year, many Silhouette readers have written in telling us what other types of stories they'd like to read from Silhouette, and we've kept these comments and suggestions in mind in developing SILHOUETTE DESIRE.

DESIREs feature all of the elements you like to see in a romance, plus a more sensual, provocative story. So if you want to experience all the excitement, passion and joy of falling in love, then SILHOUETTE DESIRE is for you.

For more details write to:

Jane Nicholls
Silhouette Books
PO Box 236
Thornton Road
Croydon
Surrey CR9 3RU

ARIEL
BERK
False
Impressions

Silhouette Desire

Originally Published by Silhouette Books
division of
Harlequin Enterprises Ltd.

First published in Great Britain 1986
by Silhouette Books, 15–16 Brook's Mews, London W1A 1DR

© Barbara Keiler 1985

Silhouette, Silhouette Desire and Colophon are Trade Marks of Harlequin Enterprises B.V.

ISBN 0 373 05239 1

22–0386

Made and printed in Great Britain by
Richard Clay (The Chaucer Press) Ltd,
Bungay, Suffolk

ARIEL BERK

is not only a novelist, she is also a composer. In her spare time she enjoys a variety of activities including sailing, sunbathing, hiking and visiting museums, but she lets nothing take too much time from her pleasure in writing.

Other Silhouette Books by Ariel Berk

Silhouette Desire

Silent Beginnings
Promise of Love
Remedies of the Heart
Hungry for Love
Breaking the Ice

*For further information about
Silhouette Books please write to:*

Jane Nicholls
Silhouette Books
PO Box 236
Thornton Road
Croydon
Surrey CR9 3RU

One

Socks," said Iris.

Audrey Lambert had watched the tall blond woman's entrance in the mirror, and now her eyes shifted from her own reflection to Iris's. Like Audrey, Iris had on the ghastly uniform that waitresses were required to wear at the Angel Club: a skimpy leotard of silver lamé with spaghetti straps, a deeply scooped neckline, and wispy wire-and-gauze wings protruding from the fabric below the shoulder blades, black mesh stockings, and high-heeled black pumps. A silver metal halo protruded from Iris's sleekly coiffed platinum hair. Audrey had been fussing with her own halo, unable to fasten it securely to the thick thatch of black curls that crowned her head.

There was no doubt that Iris looked better in the uniform than Audrey did. Iris had the build for it—sensuously broad hips, a narrow waist, and full breasts. Audrey's figure appeared thin and wan in the skintight leotard, although the high heels of her shoes gave her rear end an uncharacteristic perkiness.

"Socks?" she echoed.

Iris turned to Audrey with a smile. "It's none of my business," she admitted, "but this is your first night, and I'm only trying to be helpful. In this joint the size of your tips has a whole lot to do with the size of your bust."

"I'd love big tips," Audrey acknowledged, enunciating carefully. "But there isn't a lot I can do about my endowments at this point."

"Sure there is," Iris explained. "Socks. Where are your socks?"

Frowning, Audrey retrieved her socks from the shelf of the locker where she'd stored her street clothes. Iris plucked them from her hands, rolled each into a ball, and then stuffed them down the front of Audrey's leotard, one beneath each of Audrey's small breasts. "Pardon me for getting personal," Iris mumbled as her fingers accidentally brushed Audrey's flesh. She nudged the socks into place, then withdrew her hands. "There, that's the idea."

Audrey pivoted back to the mirror and guffawed. Augmented by the two rounded wads of her socks, her breasts appeared astonishingly voluptuous, creating a suggestive cleavage above the plunging neckline of the uniform. "Oh, God," she muttered. "This looks ridiculous."

"Honey, take it from someone who's been at the job for a year. To you and me it looks ridiculous, but to the bozos out in the dining room, it looks like heaven on earth. They're lookers, not touchers—and this is what they come here to look at. Mine are socks, too," she added boastfully, striking a modeling pose.

Audrey studied Iris's figure and then her own amplified bustline. She tried to keep a straight face as she inspected the new dimensions of her physique. "Do you really think they won't notice that this isn't me?"

"Of course. Just make sure you don't bump into something and knock the socks out of position. And use a bit more rouge, too," Iris advised. "The lighting is pretty dim out there."

Thank goodness for that, Audrey grumbled silently as she dusted a touch more of the pressed-powder blusher onto her high cheekbones. She was unused to wearing so much makeup: not only the blusher but heavy black eyeliner framing her naturally dark eyes, thick mascara stroked onto her lashes, and a crimson lipstick outlining her mouth. In general, Audrey wore little more than a tinted lip gloss. When she'd been hired by the Angel Club, she'd had to race to the drugstore to stock up on cosmetics.

All in the name of research, she reminded herself as she once again tried to attach the halo to her hair. As required by law, she had pinned her dense black curls back from her face. She suspected that the Angel Club's customers were more interested in looking than in eating and drinking, but as a waitress she had to obey the state regulations concerning workers handling food. A complete physical, clean hands, pinned hair.

Her first night working at the club hadn't yet begun, but already her back and legs ached from the unaccustomed stilt-like heels of her shoes. She sucked in her breath, unnerved by the image that flaunted femininity facing her in the mirror, the absurd leotard cut down to here and up to there and the intricate lace pattern of her hosiery. With a fortifying shrug of her shoulders, she set her makeup case in the locker with her street clothing and shut the metal door. "Any other words of wisdom for me, Iris?" she asked her colleague as they started toward the narrow corridor leading past the public rest rooms to the dining room.

"Relax and enjoy yourself," Iris suggested. "Remember, it's just a job. And the tips are better here than anywhere else I've ever worked."

Audrey didn't find that hard to believe. She'd worked as a waitress part-time during college and graduate school, and she knew that tips made up the major portion of a waitress's earnings. She also knew that as a rule, men tipped more than women, and that their tips were usually related to how attractive and deferential their waitress was. At the Angel Club, waitresses were an important part of the atmosphere. It didn't take a Ph.D. to recognize that the men who patronized the place were eager to see lots of female flesh.

She was lucky to get the job, and she was certain that her experience would be invaluable when it came to finishing her book. The bulk of the book was based on her doctoral thesis, which concerned itself with male behavior patterns in establishments like this, which were designed to cater to men's macho instincts. Her editor liked the data she'd accumulated and analyzed, but he wanted her to beef up her scholarly research with some more down-to-earth anecdotes in order for him to be able to market the book widely. At his suggestion Audrey had interviewed additional waitresses and hostesses at similar restaurants around the country, and now she was going to supplement her thesis with a little hands-on experience. She was sure that after a month or two working at the Angel Club she'd have all the experience she needed.

It was an odd position for Audrey to find herself in. By day she taught anthropology at the State University of New York at Albany. A junior faculty member, she had won the designation of the department's token feminist, the feisty scholar who specialized in what she called "male tribal rituals in America." She'd already presented several papers on such topics as "Male Conversational Tendencies in Barber Shops," "Girlie Magazines: Substance and Fluff" and "Hierarchical Order in All-Male Sports Organizations." Perhaps such subjects would have been easier for a man than a woman to research, but Audrey was brave enough to weasel her way into situations where a woman might ordinarily be out of place. She'd spent several days hiding in a broom closet at a barber shop, eavesdropping on the customers; she'd courageously purchased copies of *Playboy* and *Penthouse* magazines at the local newsstand. Now she would be witnessing firsthand the sort of interplay that went on between male patrons and female waitresses at the Angel Club.

She'd been circulating through the dimly lit main dining room delivering drinks and menus for a half hour when the hostess directed a party of four to a corner booth in Audrey's station. By now Audrey had become accustomed to the ache in her lower back caused by the ludicrously high heels of her shoes, and she set her mouth in a warm smile as she approached the round table that stood before the semicircular banquette where the four gentlemen were arranging themselves. "Good evening," she recited pleasantly. "Would you care for drinks before you order dinner?"

The men all wore neatly tailored suits, and Audrey quickly pegged them as a business group. The man seated at the end of the banquette closest to where she stood was beefy, middle-aged and beginning to bald. "Hello there, sweetie," he addressed her robustly. Audrey tried not to cringe. "I don't remember seeing you here before. Are you new?"

"Tonight's my first night," she told him, her smile causing her cheeks to cramp.

"Well, then, we'll go easy on you, won't we?" He turned to his fellow diners, and Audrey turned to them as well. The man who had spoken was the plumpest of the lot. The man beside him was considerably older, his hair white and his face lined with creases. At the far end of the banquette sat a younger man with leering eyes and a simpering grin.

The fourth man captured Audrey's attention and held it. He too was young, his hair thick and blond, somewhat longer than was stylish. His eyes were a muted blue, his skin a sun-drenched golden color, his jaw broad and square. He wore a conservative dark blue suit, and his hands were folded rigidly on the table in front of him. Audrey sensed that he felt slightly uncomfortable, though whether that was because he was squeezed onto the banquette or because of some other reason she couldn't say.

"Drinks, boys?" the plump man asked before angling his head up to Audrey. "I'll have a stinger."

"A stinger," she said with a nod, then turned to the next man on the banquette. He and the simpering young one requested martinis simultaneously. Audrey fixed her gaze on the blond man. "Would you care for a drink?" she asked.

Something in his gaze unnerved her. His eyes, she realized, were actually more gray than blue, and his lashes were a shade darker than the corn-colored hair drooping over his high brow. His lips flexed twice before he said, "What have you got in imported beers?"

Audrey listed the restaurant's selection. The man asked for a Beck's. His voice was soft and husky, much gentler than that of the plump man. She scribbled the drink order on her pad and turned toward the bar.

Before she could leave the table, the plump man reached out and slipped his arm around her waist, pulling her to his side. His words were directed to the blond man, however. "What do you say, Fox?" he asked. "Are the waitresses here spectacular or what?"

The blond man appeared embarrassed. "I'd say, Prager, that you ought to let the lady do her job," he advised his companion.

"You'd rather have a beer than look at this lovely morsel?" the plump man persisted. Audrey tried not to grimace.

"I'd rather you take your hands off her," the blond man retorted.

Under other circumstances, she would resent such protective interference from a man. It was almost as offensive as the plump man's forwardness. Audrey was fully capable of defending herself against a man's advances. But in her role as a waitress at the Angel Club, she couldn't very well slap a customer's face and tell him that if he touched her again she'd poke his eyes out. She was oddly relieved by the blond man's intercession on her behalf.

The plump man released her and offered a cloying smile. "I don't mean anything by it, honey," he apologized. "I'm harmless. Aren't I harmless?" he asked the others. The older man smiled tentatively and the leering man laughed, but the blond man remained stony-eyed.

"I'll get you your drinks," she excused herself, sidling away from the table.

At the bar she read off the order to the bartender and sighed. What had Iris said about the customers being lookers, not touchers? Well, the fat man was probably telling the truth; Audrey was certain he was harmless. Obnoxious but harmless. She wondered what was going on between him and the blond man.

The bartender filled a tray with the drinks, and Audrey braced herself with a deep breath before carrying it to the corner table. The two men seated at the ends of the banquette were chattering about something they found humorous, and the elderly man was chuckling. The blond man was the only one aware of her approach, and his eyes latched on to her when she drew to a halt and distributed the drinks and menus.

He had beautiful eyes, she decided. Gentle, soulful eyes. Too bad he was the sort of creep who dined at a restaurant like the Angel Club. "I'll be back in a few minutes to take your dinner order," she said as she set the menus down.

"Don't be too long," the plump man said to her. "I'm tempted to have you for dinner."

"I'm not on the menu," she returned, a steely hardness underlining the playful words.

"More's the pity," he complained. "What's your name, sweetheart?"

She didn't want to tell him her name, but being friendly was part of her job. "Audrey," she replied.

"Audrey. What do you say, Fox?" he called to the blond man. "Isn't Audrey worth the price?"

"Tone it down, Prager," the blond man said with barely concealed annoyance. "You're liable to make me lose my appetite."

The fat man threw back his head with a wheezy laugh. "Cheaper check. That sounds good to me." The other men laughed as well, and Audrey departed from the table.

Delivering a round of dinners to another table, she was keenly attuned to the quartet at the corner table—in particular, to the quiet blond man in their midst. She reminded herself that as a customer at the Angel Club, the blond man was definitely not the sort of person she had much respect for. She glided through the smoky dining room, its walls covered in burgundy foil paper with veins of silver running through it, and its floors blanketed in carpeting thick enough to muffle her footsteps; she checked on another table and brought over a second basket of rolls. Yet she felt those relentless gray-blue eyes on her even when she was halfway across the room. They followed her, watching her weave among the tables, watching the reflexive sway of her hips as she balanced on her high heels.

If anyone was ogling her, the blond man was, and she was irked by it. He didn't seem like the ogling type. But then, if he wasn't, what was he doing here? Men came to the Angel Club to look, and the man named Fox was definitely looking.

She distracted herself from her resentment by recalling the importance of her current job to her book. Teaching four courses at the university as well as waitressing Thursday through Sunday nights was certain to wear her down. She'd be wise not to waste any of her precious energy by fuming about the blond man's persistent staring.

When she returned to the corner table to take the men's dinner orders, the plump man refrained from teasing her, and all four of the men announced their dinner choices without incident. If the blond man was more conscious of Audrey than she felt comfortable about, she managed not to let her anger get the better of her. She simply gathered the menus and swept away from the table, heading directly for the kitchen.

As she waited for one of the assistant chefs to garnish the entrees for another of her tables, she used the pause to reflect on her indignation about the foursome at the corner table. If she should be angry with any of them, it ought to be with the plump man, she mused. He was the one who'd slung his arm around her, called her "sweetie," flirted shamelessly with her. Yet that sort of behavior seemed appropriate for him. He was ruddy-faced, over-bearing, obviously a regular at the club. She'd expect such silliness from the likes of him. According to the data she'd accumulated in her several years of research, he was the archetypical patron of girlie-type restaurants: past his prime physically, probably married—she made a mental note to spy on his left hand in search of a ring—coy and imagining himself to be full of charm. His manner was an adult version of the behavior of kindergarten children trading bathroom jokes on the playground.

He was what she expected. The blond man wasn't. Again she found herself wondering about his relationship to the plump man. Perhaps he was a subordinate and had had no vote in where they'd adjourn for dinner. She hoped that was the case.

But why should she even care? Why should she give a hoot about him?

Entering the dining room with her tray of dinner plates, she immediately felt his eyes on her again, and his con-stant gaze caused a chill to crawl through her flesh. Just because the man was attractive didn't allow her to forgive him for gaping so blatantly at her sock-upholstered bust-line, at her painted eyes and cherry-red lips.

When she delivered dinner to the four men, they were engrossed in a heated discussion, something to do with a pending trial. Lawyers, she pondered with a silent sniff. According to her profile of regular customers at restau-rants like the Angel Club, such men were frequently professionals. Not surprising, since such restaurants tended to be high-priced. The Angel Club definitely was.

The demands of her job kept her from dwelling on the blond man at the corner table. She tried to remember whether her past work as a waitress had rendered her as fatigued as she was by ten-thirty. Of course, she had been younger then, though at twenty-nine years of age she wasn't exactly old. But at those previous jobs she'd been allowed to wear comfortable shoes. She was convinced that her high heels were chiefly responsible for her weariness.

Certain that her customers were taken care of for the moment, she slipped out of the dining room and down the hall to the dressing room reserved for the waitresses. Closing the door behind her, she kicked off her shoes and groaned. She bent at the waist and let her shoulders sag toward the floor. Her first night on the job, and already she was praying for closing time to arrive. *All in the name of research,* she once again whispered to herself.

She touched up her makeup at the mirror, rearranged her socks beneath her breasts, and tried futilely to make her halo stand straight above her scalp. With another groan, she jammed her tender feet back into her shoes and left the locker room.

Just as she passed the men's bathroom, the door swung wide and the blond man emerged, bumping into her. She hastily glanced at her chest to make sure the socks were still in place, then lifted her eyes to him.

He stood half a head above her, which, given the height of her shoes, put him at about six feet tall. His body was lean, the impeccable lines of his dark suit flattering his lanky physique. His necktie was loosened, the collar of his white button-down shirt open. His jawline hinted at a faint stubble of beard. In the brightly lit hallway, his hair seemed even lighter to her, a straight, recently combed sheet of gold.

"Excuse me," he murmured, drawing a step back from her.

She smiled—a significant part of her job entailed always smiling at the customers—and said, "No problem."

His eyes coursed over her, wandering down from the thick dark mop of her hair to the even features of her face, the large, widely set eyes, the aquiline nose, the vividly painted lips, and further down to her slender shoulders, her taut cleavage, her dark seductive hosiery. "Audrey, is it?" he asked.

It dawned on her that he might be planning to make a pass at her, and she quickly prepared herself for such an eventuality. She would have preferred to deal with the plump man in this circumstance, or either of the other men in their party—or any other man she'd served that evening. From them she'd expect a come-on; from them she could fend it off with ease. But this man was too...attractive, she admitted to herself.

Too attractive, but no better than the others. Just another oily customer gawking at female flesh for an evening. "I've got to get back to work," she said, forcing a smile.

He hesitated, but refused to step out of her way in the narrow corridor. "My name is Brandon Fox," he told her.

Did he think that his name made any difference to her? Her smile grew progressively more artificial as she tried to edge past him.

He reached for her arm, but she shrank back before he could touch her. His hand dropped limply to his side. "What time do you get off?" he asked.

Forget it, buddy, she muttered internally. *Not interested in the least.* But her job required her to remain congenial, and she mumbled, "The club closes at one o'clock."

"Can I meet you afterward?"

Despite having expected the question, she felt a hot twinge running along her spine at the enticing huskiness of his voice. Her resentment directed itself inward. She'd never been the sort of woman to be intrigued by a man simply because he was remarkably handsome, or because his voice was soft and sensuous. In general, she didn't harbor much trust in men at all—and surely not in the kind of men one met at places like the Angel Club. Still, she clung to her waitress etiquette and said gently, "I'm sorry—we're not allowed to date customers." In fact, she didn't think the restaurant had any such rule, but it seemed like a tactful way of discouraging the man's attentions.

"After one o'clock I wouldn't be a customer," he pointed out, then paused, frowning slightly. "Or would I?"

His implication was clear, and she smothered the urge to slap him. This job was going to be hazardous if she kept wanting to slap her customers, she thought as she fought for self-control. In a falsely sweet voice, she said, "I probably should pretend you didn't say that, Mr. Fox. Why don't you rejoin your party?"

"I'd rather look at you," he replied.

A looker, but not nearly as harmless as his pudgy associate at the table. Far more obnoxious, and by no stretch of the imagination harmless. Audrey shifted restlessly from foot to foot, the hot twinge Brandon Fox had evoked replaced by a gnawing ache at the small of her back. "What you'd rather look at isn't my concern," she said, unable to contain the testiness in her tone. "And what I do after closing time isn't your concern. Please leave me alone." When she again attempted to pass him, he stepped out of her path, and she fled to the dark dining room. *There goes my tip from him,* she grumbled as she skirted the corner table to present the bill to a neighboring party of three.

She noticed Brandon Fox returning to his table and chastised herself for being so painfully conscious of him.

She wished he had a nasal voice; she wished his eyes were crossed. She wished he'd done something so utterly offensive that her rage at him would be fully justified. She wished she'd had the guts to slap him.

He's a creep, she firmly reminded herself. His very presence in the Angel Club marked him as a creep. He attended a place like this not because he respected women and considered them his equals but for quite the opposite reason: because he wanted to gawk at flesh. She recalled the way his eyes focused on the neckline of her uniform, the way they briefly played down the length of her slender legs, which appeared even longer than they were due to the high cut of the leotard on her outer thighs and the stiletto heels of her shoes. Youth and good looks notwithstanding, the man was a lecher.

The fat man at the corner table signaled her for the check, and she swallowed and defiantly raised her chin before approaching with the prepared bill. "I hope you enjoyed your meal," she mumbled, looking anywhere but at Brandon Fox.

"Tremendously," the plump man boomed as he removed a credit card from his wallet. "What do you say, boys? Is it unanimous?"

The older man and the simpering man both concurred enthusiastically, but Brandon Fox said nothing. His eyes remained on Audrey as she gathered up the card and carried the bill away. His continuous stare made the skin at the back of her neck prickle. She loathed him, she decided. He was clearly the worst of the lot, suave and subtle where they were obvious, yet more than willing to corner her privately and make his desires known.

What nerve, she continued to simmer even after the four men left the restaurant. What nerve! Insinuating that she was a prostitute, that he might still be her customer if they met after hours! What in the world did he think she was? Just because her uniform was offensively revealing didn't make her a tart. She was a waitress—at least, at the Angel Club, she was—and he had some incredible gall implying that she was anything more than that. She was a waitress and this was a job. Even the research on girlie restaurants she'd conducted in graduate school hadn't had the impact on her that Brandon Fox's slimy behavior had. Hands-on experience indeed! She could write an entire chapter of her book on the feeling of debasement a waitress suffered while working in a joint like the Angel Club.

Her fury invigorated her, making her forget about the soreness in her back and ankles, making her ignore the occasionally suggestive comments other diners tossed her way. That her anger with Brandon Fox was far out of proportion to his actions didn't lessen it. He was disgusting, she decided. Sleazy, slimy, disrespectful, despicable Disgusting.

As the last few diners were ushered out of the restaurant at closing time, Audrey stormed to the locker room, eager to shed her uniform and don her comfortable civilian clothing: jeans, a baggy wool sweater, a denim jacket against the brisk autumn chill. Two of the other waitresses were already changing their clothes as Audrey entered, and Iris soon joined them. "How'd your first night go?" she asked Audrey.

"All right," Audrey conceded grudgingly, yanking the pins from her hair and letting the black curls tumble to her shoulders.

"What's the matter?" Iris asked, accurately reading Audrey's agitated mood as she joined her at the counter below the mirror and methodically peeled off her false eyelashes. "Lousy tips?"

"No, excellent tips," Audrey admitted. In fact the generous tips she'd received had amazed her.

"Then, what?" Iris pressed her.

"Just tired," Audrey said with a sigh. "These shoes are awful. I'm going to wind up in a body cast before the end of the month."

"You'll get used to it," Iris assured her. She wiped off her makeup with a baby-oil-soaked cotton ball. "Come on, what happened? Did some guy give you a rough time?"

Audrey shrugged. She pulled off the leotard, then bent to retrieve her socks from the floor where they'd dropped. "As a matter of fact, yes," she muttered.

"It happens," Iris said sympathetically. "The minute they walk in the door, they forget their manners. They figure if we can put up with these silly uniforms we can put up with anything."

"Men," Audrey grunted. She bit her lip to stifle herself. She knew enough about the way men exploited women from the example of her father, a man who claimed to be liberal and open-minded but whose behavior toward his wife and only child—whose gender had sorely disappointed him—had always been contemptuous and repressive. Audrey's father squelched her mother whenever she tried to assert herself, whenever she made the merest signs of wanting an independent life. And although her mother never knew about them, Audrey was painfully aware of her father's infidelities. When, years ago, she'd finally had the guts to confront him about his affairs, he'd explained that women were either wives and mothers or they were tramps, and that any sensible man knew the difference and acted on that knowledge.

Audrey wanted to believe that her father was wrong, but the world seemed determined to prove him right. No matter how many women stormed the barricades, demanding equality and respect, most men went on blithely dividing womankind into madonnas and whores, and treating them accordingly. A woman who worked at the Angel Club, in her scant uniform and her coquettish halo, obviously couldn't be a madonna. Therefore a man felt he had the right to suggest that if he saw her after hours he'd still be her customer.

Audrey tried to put Brandon Fox and his insufferably degrading remark out of her mind as she fastened her bra and then yanked her bulky sweater over her head. She shook her curls loose, then shrugged on her jacket and hoisted her helmet from the floor of the locker. "I'll see you all tomorrow," she said as she headed for the door.

"Don't let it get to you," Iris called after her. "It's just a job."

Audrey nodded and managed a feeble smile before leaving the dressing room.

The night air was cool and refreshing after the stuffy atmosphere of the restaurant, and the sky was clear and punctuated with glimmering stars. Audrey felt her tension waning as she ambled across the parking lot to her motor scooter. She hoisted her knapsack, which contained her uniform and wallet, onto her shoulders and straddled the small motorbike, eager to get home, shower and crawl into bed. Settling herself on the bike's saddle, she detected a movement in the shadows of the lot's perimeter, the silhouette of a man. She instantly gauged the distance back to the restaurant, wondering if she should make a dash for safety.

He emerged from behind a car, calling her name. "Audrey?"

Oh, Lord, it's Fox, she moaned soundlessly. Even in the night's gloom his hair glistened a golden blond. He strolled toward her, and her hands reflexively gripped the handle-bars. She should have gotten her key from the pocket of her jeans, she mused, so she could career out of the lot and leave him in a cloud of dust. But for some reason she was unable to release the handlebars to get her key. Her fingers curled tightly about the handles, shaping fists.

"Audrey, I'm sorry about what I said before," Brandon murmured, discreetly leaving several feet of asphalt between them.

"And I'm *not* sorry about what I said," she retorted. "It's closing time. I'm going home."

"Audrey...look, I don't know what you think of me—"

"You don't *want* to know," she cut him off.

His hands were plunged into the pockets of his slacks, but he seemed oblivious to the cold. A light breeze lifted his hair from his brow. His eyes were uncommonly clear and alert, given the hour. "I find you very attractive," he said, his tone soft but forthright.

"So what do you want, a medal?" she snapped. "Listen, mister—"

"Brandon Fox," he reintroduced himself.

She wished she could plug her ears. She didn't want to think of him in terms of a name. She didn't want to think of him as a human being. He was just a man, a lecherous man. "What you were so attracted to in there wasn't me," she explained tautly, mildly amused by the irony of the statement. After all, what he was attracted to in the restaurant was a spy behind enemy lines, an incognito college professor gathering information for a book that might ultimately lead to tenure. What she said, however, was, "It was a waitress in a ridiculous getup. Go home and have a sweet dream, Fox. I'm not interested."

"*I'm* interested," he persisted, his voice wavering slightly. "I'm not sure why, but I am."

"What do you mean, you're not sure why?" She laughed. "How old are you? You don't know why you were interested? It's called pulchritude, buster. It's called Flesh City. It's called the fantasies of a little boy. But the fantasy ends at one A.M. So leave me alone."

He remained standing on the asphalt, scrutinizing her. His eyes seemed to reflect confusion and doubt, and Audrey laughed again. For heaven's sake, he was acting like someone who'd just emerged from a jungle where he'd been raised by apes, and didn't understand his own very human, very masculine urges. Show a man a woman with long legs and cleavage and of course he's going to be interested. If Brandon Fox didn't know that, he must be an idiot.

Fox, she contemplated, her fisted hands relaxing enough for her to retrieve the key to her motorbike. She inserted it into the ignition and smothered another chuckle. What a perfect name, she mused. Fox. Pretending to be slow on the uptake, but there was no question in her mind that he was a fox, as sly and cunning as they came.

With a sputtering cough the motor ignited. She revved it, then released the brake and whisked out of the lot, her rear tire kicking pebbles in Brandon Fox's direction. Just what he deserves, she thought, satisfaction replacing her annoyance. A hail of pebbles burying the Fox in his own fantasies. The perfect comeuppance for a man like him.

Two

What had he expected? Not a motorbike.

After dusting off his trousers, he slowly crossed the lot to his Volvo and climbed behind the wheel. He rolled down the window to allow some of the brisk October air into the car's interior, then slouched in the bucket seat and shook his head. What had he expected?

He supposed her indignation was justified, given his inappropriate comment in the hallway by the rest room. But...but he didn't know how to behave around women like Audrey. When he'd confronted her in the parking lot, he'd tried to explain, tried to apologize. He'd been truthful, as truthful as he always was. Brandon didn't lie to women; he didn't play games.

He'd never actually talked to someone like Audrey before. Not that he'd lived a sheltered life, but waitresses in places like the Angel Club were not the sort of people he generally socialized with. His unexpected attraction to Audrey disturbed him.

Brandon liked to think of himself as a liberated man. He enjoyed cooking, he did his own laundry, he fetched coffee for himself at the office rather than asking one of the secretaries to get it for him. He prided himself on his interest in women as equals, as human beings. His manhood was never wounded when a woman asked him out, paid for dinner, took the initiative sexually. Brandon was glad to be alive now, when women had attained such a measure of independence. He wouldn't have functioned well in a society where he would be expected to make all the decisions, issue all the orders, earn all the money for some fragile, helpless woman who spent her days making herself pretty for him and her nights carrying him his slippers and attending to his every whim.

So why had he reacted to Audrey the way he had? She was totally unlike the sort of women who usually attracted him. Much too much makeup, for one thing, and her figure...awfully top-heavy. He preferred a slim, athletic build on a woman, not an overly buxom figure like Audrey's.

Then, what? What was it about her? Something in her eyes, perhaps, something in those large dark eyes of hers that spoke of things beyond the Kewpie-doll image she presented in her tawdry angel outfit. Something in the velvety softness of her voice. Something in the way her anger had lit up her face....

He shook his head again and started the car's engine. It was late; he was confused. Maybe in the morning it would make sense to him.

His confusion as he drove through the dark, nearly empty streets of Albany was laced with impatience. He hadn't paid as much attention to Prager over dinner as he ought to have, and he was sure Thornton would criticize him about it Monday morning. But wasn't it just like Prager to choose a place like the Angel Club to discuss business?

Brandon suspected that little would have been accomplished over dinner even if he hadn't been so distracted by Audrey. His clients were determined to go to trial, and he didn't think that behind-the-scenes negotiating with Prager would do much good. Brandon worked for a law firm that specialized in civil rights cases, and the current case he was assigned to, a class-action suit brought by a group of women to end discrimination against females at the exclusive Capital Club, was typical of the sort of cases Thornton-Lapidas-McGuff accepted.

Prager, who represented the Capital Club, worked for a much larger firm, but Brandon wasn't daunted by Prager's resources. When he'd graduated from law school, Brandon had been courted by firms like Prager's, but instead he'd bucked the tide and taken a job with the small but prestigious Thornton-Lapidas-McGuff in Albany, where he could ply his knowledge on the sort of cases where he believed true justice was best served: discrimination suits, environmental disputes, First Amendment fights. He could have earned more money elsewhere, but he was content where he was, and challenged by his assignments.

He arrived at the renovated brownstone where he lived in a part of the city that had recently undergone gentrification. After locking the car, he climbed the stairs to his second-floor apartment. A former girlfriend had helped him to decorate the spacious, high-ceilinged rooms—not because Brandon believed that women were better than men at decorating homes but because he himself simply hadn't known how to go about doing it.

He really wasn't sexist, he tried to reassure himself. He really was a high-minded man. So why the hell had he been so turned on by Audrey?

Her dark eyes haunted him as he stalked down the hall to his bedroom and clicked on the lamp by his bed. He undressed, washed and slid beneath the down quilt, then shut the light off. In the room's darkness he tried to blot out the picture he had of her in his mind, her lovely face slathered with all that garish paint, her huge breasts straining at the fabric of her uniform, her long, beautifully proportioned legs... "Damn!" he muttered aloud. He felt like a slobbering adolescent, the kind of kid who thought with his glands and papered his walls with pin-ups. This was not at all like Brandon Fox.

He didn't sleep well. His dreams were filled with Audrey's striking eyes, the vulnerable curve of her lips, the delicate shadows cast by her collarbones against the silky skin of her upper chest. Maybe some urges couldn't be civilized out of a man, he thought morosely.

Arising at dawn, he pulled on his sweatsuit and took a long, energizing run. When he returned to the apartment he showered and ate a light breakfast, then organized himself for baking bread. Baking bread was something he enjoyed, and he tried to bake a loaf every weekend so he could savor it through the week. Some of his male colleagues teased him about his culinary skill, but he let their playful mocking bounce off him. In this day and age there was nothing wrong with a man's knowing how to bake.

But today the baking didn't bring him its usual pleasure. He knew he was only doing it to keep himself too busy to think about Audrey.

At noon his telephone rang. "Bran? It's Karen," the caller identified herself.

Karen was an associate of Brandon's at the firm, and one of his closest friends. If they hadn't worked together—and if she hadn't already been happily married—he might have pursued a deeper relationship with her. As it was, he was genuinely fond of her husband, and Brandon's relationship with Karen was akin to a brother-sister closeness.

Karen had wanted to be assigned to the Capital Club case, but Thornton had vetoed it. "Given the nature of the suit," he'd proclaimed, "I think we're best off letting it be handled by men. If we wind up going to jury, our case will look stronger if the jurors see men defending women's rights." Although Karen had been disappointed, she had accepted Thornton's decision.

"Hi, Karen," Brandon greeted his friend. Simply hearing her voice heartened him. Karen was bright, well-educated, professional—the sort of woman he felt comfortable with. "What's up?"

"What's up is I'm all by my lonesome," she announced. "Tim has to spend the weekend at his parents' house in Boston."

"Oh?"

"Crisis time," Karen said with a sigh. "My sister-in-law announced she's getting a divorce, so the entire family has been summoned to the compound to fuss about it."

"How come you didn't go?"

Karen snorted. "My in-laws hate me," she reminded Brandon. She'd often complained to him about how her husband's family disapproved of her ambition, her desire to pursue her own career rather than to become a homemaker upon marrying Tim. "This was one visit I was more than happy to pass up. So, I'm free tonight. Are you?"

"As a matter of fact, yes," Brandon answered. "What's the plan?"

"I thought we could get together for dinner and you could tell me all about the Capital Club case. You and Thornton were out with Prager and his lackey last night, weren't you? I want a full report."

There wasn't much to report, but Brandon was pleased by Karen's invitation. An evening with her might erase from his mind thoughts about Audrey. "Sounds great," he agreed. "Since you're all by your lonesome, I'll treat."

"I won't argue," Karen chirped. "Pick me up at six."

"Okay. I'll see you then," said Brandon before hanging up.

He read the newspaper while his dough rose the first time, and perused his Capital Club file for the umpteenth time while the dough rose the second time. As he puttered around his kitchen and his office-den, he tried to focus on the evening he'd be spending with Karen. Yet even their impending dinner couldn't dislodge troubling thoughts about Audrey from his mind.

What was it about her, he asked himself again and again. Maybe that was the wrong question, he reasoned. Maybe he ought to be asking what it was about himself that made him respond to such a stridently sexy woman. Did an untamed animal lurk beneath his genteel exterior?

He couldn't believe that of himself. After all, he hadn't given a second look to any of the other scantily clad waitresses at the Angel Club. And it wasn't Audrey's sex appeal that had captivated him. Once more he reminded himself that she was too buxom, that her mask of makeup was too thick for his taste. But maybe that was simply so much self-justifying, he argued. Maybe his ability to bake bread, his willingness to iron his shirts, his seemingly easy camaraderie with women were all a pose. Maybe beneath his cultivated veneer he *was* just another drooling male animal.

His analytical brain failed him. The bread baked beautifully, but Brandon could make no sense of his feelings for Audrey. Whenever he thought about her, whenever he pictured her, he felt a dark stirring deep within him, some primitive attraction he couldn't understand. Lust, he thought disdainfully. *Call it like it is, Fox. You've got the hots for a chesty broad. Don't deny it.*

At five he shaved, then dressed in a gray tweed sports jacket and gray flannel slacks. He hadn't yet decided where he would take Karen; although it was his treat, he'd thought he'd let her choose the restaurant.

He drove to the house she and Tim owned north of the state university campus. Karen bounded down the front walk as soon as he drew to a stop in the driveway. She looked lovely, he decided, her straight brown hair curved in a perfect pageboy and her slender figure flattered by a neat shirtwaist dress. Karen had the kind of clean good looks that generally appealed to Brandon. "Hi," she hailed him, letting herself into the car. "I just got off the phone with Tim. God, am I glad I'm not in Boston with him. He said he's already downed half a bottle of aspirin."

"A suicide attempt, or just a whopping headache?" Brandon asked as he backed into the street.

"I didn't bother to ask," Karen said with an impish shrug. "Poor boy. He'll be a basket case by the time he gets home tomorrow. So, Bran, where are we going?"

"I thought I'd leave that up to you," Brandon offered, coasting to a halt at the corner to give her a chance to decide on a restaurant.

"Hmm." She shrugged again. "I don't care. Someplace where you can tell me all about Prager and his precious Capital Club case. I don't like the man," she muttered. "I'm almost glad I wasn't assigned to the case.

If I ever had to face him in court, I'd be tempted to string him up by his thumbs.''

"Shame, shame," said Brandon, clicking his tongue. Then he laughed. "You'll never guess where he took us last night for dinner."

"Where?" Karen asked eagerly.

"The Angel Club."

"That hoochie-koochie joint on Pearl Street?" Karen exclaimed, then shuddered. "Don't they have topless waitresses there?"

"Not quite," Brandon told her. "Actually, it's not really a joint. The food wasn't bad, and the waitresses..." His voice drifted for a moment, and he cleared his throat. "Their uniforms are on the tacky side, Karen, but they aren't topless. I'll grant you, Pragar showed a definite lack of sensitivity in taking us there to discuss the Capital Club case, but, no, it wasn't as bad as you've heard."

"Sure," Karen muttered, unconvinced. "I bet it's as bad as the Capital Club. I bet they won't let women customers in there, either."

"Do you want to find out?" Brandon asked impulsively.

As soon as he spoke he regretted the suggestion. But it was too late. He could see Karen's eyes glowing with anticipation of the fight she'd wage at the door if the hostess refused to admit her into the place. If Brandon knew Karen—and he did—she probably was hoping they'd bar her just so she could raise a ruckus.

"Let's go," she said emphatically. "I want to see these topless waitresses for myself. If Tim can pop off to Boston for a weekend without me, I deserve some fun."

"Tim isn't having fun," Brandon pointed out.

"Then I'll have enough fun for both of us," Karen resolved. "Drive on, Bran. The Angel Club it is."

Brandon shifted into gear and steered east toward Pearl Street. The more he considered it, the more he realized that taking Karen to the Angel Club was a foolish idea. It wasn't merely that she was itching for a fight; he didn't really think she'd be barred from entering the restaurant, though he couldn't recall whether any women had been eating there last night. He'd been conscious of only one woman in the entire place: Audrey.

That, he admitted silently, was why he was reluctant to return to the restaurant. He wasn't sure he was ready to see Audrey again. Especially not with Karen present. Audrey might misinterpret their relationship and assume that Karen was more than just Brandon's friend. And Karen...what if she noticed his awkwardness around Audrey? She'd give him hell for having taken a fancy to a flashy lady like Audrey.

But Karen was dead set on the Angel Club for dinner, and as Brandon dolefully parked in the lot beside the restaurant he inhaled deeply and determined to make the best of things. Perhaps seeing Audrey while he was in Karen's company would bring his feelings into focus, and help him to come back to his senses.

"This isn't so bad," Karen commented, sounding oddly deflated as the hostess, who wore a relatively demure gown of diaphanous white material with glittering silver threads running through it, asked if they had a reservation and then escorted them to a small table at the center of the dim dining room. Brandon was tempted to suggest that now that Karen had proven that female clientele was welcome at the club, they ought to leave. But Karen was already seating herself and surveying the room, studying the waitresses who circulated among the tables in their strange costumes.

"You were hoping for topless, huh," Brandon teased, his gaze also drifting about the room, instinctively searching for Audrey.

A tall blond waitress approached their table, and Brandon felt mildly relieved that Audrey wouldn't be serving them. He and Karen ordered drinks, and then Karen turned back to him. "So tell me about last night. What did Prager have to say?"

"Just what I expected he'd say," Brandon related. "He boasted about how the Capital Club doesn't discriminate against minorities. He ran through the membership list as if it were a veritable U.N.: they had blacks, Jews, people of Polish extraction, Orientals, Puerto Ricans, two Sikh Hindus. Even a few token Wasps, he bragged. That's his idea of funny," Brandon explained with a scowl. "His point was that women aren't a minority, so we can't accuse the Capital Club of discriminating against minorities. Then he did a song and dance about the nature of private clubs and the dangers of judicial interference, and he said his clients would be willing to swear on a stack of Bibles that no business was ever discussed at the place, so women couldn't contend that they were being excluded from important business opportunities."

"And you said...?"

Brandon scowled again. He hadn't said much, actually, Thornton had done most of the talking. "Thornton and I explained that even if business wasn't literally discussed at the club—which we of course don't believe—vital connections and friendships are fostered there. Then we romped through the tax issue—the club's tax exemption as a private nonprofit establishment means that women are subsidizing a club whose benefits they can't partake in." He fell silent as the waitress delivered their drinks, then concluded, "There's little question in my mind that we're headed to trial. I think the plaintiffs are especially fired up because the Capital Club is such an old, venerable institution."

"I don't blame them," Karen asserted. "The only reason I wouldn't want to join the club is that it's not the sort of place that serves people like you and me. I'm better off paying my dues to the American Civil Liberties Union. But Tim would benefit from joining a place like that, being in banking and all. And he won't join because women are banned and he thinks that's wrong. So we're being hurt by the club's policy. I'd love to see that doddering bastion of chauvinism brought to its knees."

"Don't lecture me," Brandon protested with a chuckle. "I'm on your side."

Abruptly his vision filled with Audrey, who was carrying a tray to a table not far from them, and he sucked in his breath. She looked the same tonight as she had last night, her face caked with unnecessary makeup, her figure overwhelmed by her large breasts, her wavy hair haphazardly pinned beneath her lopsided halo. But as with last night, it was her eyes that captured his attention and held it. So large, so profoundly dark, glimmering with unreadable emotions. After depositing the items on her tray she straightened up, and her gaze locked onto his. Her eyes widened in surprise, and the corners of her lips turned downward with distaste.

Evidently she wasn't pleased to see him, Brandon mused. But why should she be? He'd been a crass boor last night, and she hadn't given him a chance to explain...to explain what? That he was just another little boy with big fantasies? She hadn't needed him to explain that.

"What?" Karen sensed his sudden discomfort. She traced the angle of his eyes to Audrey, who stood immobile some twenty-five feet from them, gaping at Brandon. "Who's that?"

"Last night's waitress," Brandon mumbled, twisting away from Audrey and concentrating on the menu.

Karen continued to stare at Audrey until she pivoted on her heel and marched into the kitchen. Then Karen turned fully to Brandon. "Why was she gawking at you like that?"

"Beats me," he lied. "I think I'll try the braised duckling tonight. The roast beef was good, in case you're interested."

"What I'm interested in," Karen said, leaning forward, "is why that waitress was shooting daggers at you with her eyes."

Brandon lowered his menu and groaned. He was a terrible liar, and he certainly couldn't lie to his good friend. "I think she hates me," he confessed.

"I gathered as much," Karen noted. "How come?"

"We had kind of an unfortunate run-in last night," he revealed evasively.

He was temporarily spared from explaining further when their waitress arrived to take their orders, but once she was gone again, Karen riveted her attention to Brandon. "An unfortunate run-in? Do fill me in—I'm all ears."

Brandon groaned again, then decided to confide in his friend. Perhaps she could talk some sanity back into him. "Karen," he began hesitantly, then forged ahead. "I asked her if I could see her after hours."

"Her?" Karen scanned the dining room and located Audrey at another table. She examined her thoughtfully, then shifted back to Brandon. "You asked *her* out? She isn't your type, Bran."

"I know," he agreed. "At least I *thought* I knew, until last night. Karen, there's something about her that's gotten to me. I don't know what, or why, but—"

"Her proportions," Karen guessed disdainfully. "Bran, I'm surprised at you. You've never been the sort to go gaga over a pair of humongous knockers."

He winced. "I know. It's awful," he moaned.

Karen began to laugh. "So what happened during this unfortunate run-in?" she prodded him.

He shuddered. "I inadvertantly implied that she was a prostitute."

"Oh, Brandon!" Karen appeared indignant on Audrey's behalf. "How could you?"

"I was out of my depth," he rationalized. "She's a painted woman. What do I know about painted women?"

"Good God, just because she's overdone it with rouge and lipstick doesn't mean you had to insult her that way," Karen rose to Audrey's defense. "I'm ashamed of you."

"I'm ashamed of myself," he admitted. "I tried to apologize to her, Karen, but she refused to listen to me."

"Well, you'll just have to try again," Karen resolved. Before Brandon could stop her, she signaled to their waitress. "Excuse me," she requested, "but could you tell that dark-haired waitress over there that this gentleman wishes to speak to her?"

The blond waitress peered over her shoulder. "Audrey? Sure, I'll get her," she complied.

Brandon watched the waitress's departure with increasing dread. "Why the hell did you do that?" he muttered to Karen.

"Because you owe her an apology," Karen maintained. "Just because she works here doesn't mean you can treat her with disrespect. We sisters have to stick up for each other."

Great, Brandon mumbled under his breath. He'd known Karen was thirsting for a good fight. If she couldn't have one with the restaurant's management, she had to vent her firebrand instincts some other way.

He avoided meeting Audrey's eyes as she approached the table. When she arrived, he found his vision even with her breasts and hastily glanced away. "Hello, Audrey," he murmured, his gaze fixed on his napkin.

"What do you want?" she asked, looking from Brandon to Karen and frowning.

Karen stared reproachfully at Brandon, and he bravely raised his face to Audrey. Again he was transfixed by her eyes, their inviting darkness drawing him in. "I want to apologize for last night," he said, the words coming surprisingly easily to him.

"Let's just forget it," she grumbled.

"No," he insisted, suddenly eager to make her recognize that he wasn't as crude as he'd seemed yesterday. "No, let's not forget it, Audrey. I said a horrible thing and I'm sorry."

"What horrible thing did you say?" she goaded sarcastically. "Something about how you couldn't imagine why you were attracted to me?"

Karen's hazel eyes flickered with interest, but Brandon resolutely ignored her. "That was the truth," he countered. "I *am* attracted to you. I'm not sure why, but I am."

"Cripes!" Audrey erupted. "Here you are, sitting in front of your girlfriend and speaking to me this way! Where did you learn how to act, in the gutter? I don't believe this!"

Karen giggled. "No," she interjected. "I'm not his—"

"Karen is just a friend," Brandon said steadily. "It was her idea that I try to apologize for what I said."

"Kinky." Audrey sniffed. "I'm not interested."

Karen's laughter grew stronger. "No, Audrey," she endeavored to explain. "I'm really not his girlfriend. I'm married, for heaven's sake."

Audrey stared. "This is too sordid for me," she snorted. "Excuse me. I've got work to do." She stormed away from the table, refusing Brandon a farewell look.

He turned irritably to Karen. "Thanks a heap," he complained.

"Now, Bran, you can't blame her for being insulted."

"But I can blame you for butting in. Why did you have to do that? Now I look even worse to her."

Karen's smile faded as she appraised her friend. "What's with you, Bran? You're really stuck on her."

"No, I'm not," he protested. "I'm just..." He wasn't sure what he was, but whatever it was, it probably wasn't just. He *was* stuck on the loose-looking woman with what Karen had herself insultingly labeled humongous knockers. He was stuck on her, and, if anything, their latest dialogue had only complicated matters even more.

"Okay," Karen declared, bending toward Brandon. "Do you want my advice?"

"No!" he vehemently replied.

Karen went on, undeterred. "Send her some flowers. Send her a little note telling her you were way out of line, and you want to show her what a gentleman you are, and attach it to a big bouquet of flowers."

Brandon grimaced. "Oh, come on, Karen. That's so old-fashioned."

"Maybe she's an old-fashioned woman," Karen suggested.

Brandon glanced toward Audrey, who was taking an order at a distant table, and his grimace deepened. "An old-fashioned woman? Dressed like that?" He shook his head. "Admit it, Karen, if Tim ever sent you a big bouquet of flowers you'd think he was an unreconstructed Neanderthal.''

"Either that or I'd assume he was having an affair," Karen concurred. "But your waitress friend is different from me. She seems like just the kind of woman who'd respond to flowers. Take it from a woman. I've got an intuition about her. She may be different from me, but I bet flowers would do the trick."

"She's different enough from you that you're in no position to tell me how to deal with her," Brandon argued. He toyed with his drink, his thoughts swirling in his skull. Maybe Karen was on to something, he contemplated. He'd never courted women with flowers and candy and charm before, but then, he'd never courted a woman like Audrey before. He was so used to dealing with upscale liberated women that he felt like a beginner when it came to an extremely feminine woman like Audrey. Maybe flowers were the best strategy. She'd never be able to consider flowers kinky or sordid.

The waitress brought their dinners, and as Brandon picked at his food he meditated about Audrey, about her unnerving appeal. She might be extremely feminine, but she had a backbone of steel. She was as feisty and stubborn as Karen, as any of the women whom Brandon associated with. The only real difference was her profession, he mused, her profession and the revealing attire she wore when she worked.

He tried to concoct a suitable story about how she'd ended up toiling as a waitress at the Angel Club. She could be an unwed mother, abandoned by some heartless man, working at the only job she was able to get in order to keep her child well-fed. Maybe she had a cruel father; maybe she'd had to leave school and run away from home, and waitressing was the only sort of employment she was trained for. He simply didn't want to believe that she'd chosen to work at the Angel Club because she liked waving the upper portion of her anatomy beneath the noses of leering swine. Brandon had too much respect for women to think that they'd deliberately elect to expose their bodies to men the way they did at the Angel Club.

Fortunately, Karen remained subdued over dinner. Brandon figured that her silly adventure with Audrey had satisfied her desire for a showdown. He was furious with her for having interfered, yet he couldn't discount everything she'd said. Although she was a cultured, well-educated attorney, she was also Audrey's "sister," a woman with intuitions. Possibly she understood another woman far better than Brandon ever could.

Indeed, his understanding of women was severely shaken. He had expected Karen to berate him for finding a woman like Audrey attractive, and instead she'd leaped to Audrey's defense. As far as his understanding of Audrey...what little he understood wasn't enough. He'd said the one thing he ought never to have said, and everything he said thereafter was tainted in her eyes. It wasn't that she was eager for his respect. Quite the opposite—*he* was eager for *her* respect, and if the only way he could earn it was with flowers, he shouldn't reject the idea out of hand.

Flowers. Roses perhaps. Long-stemmed American Beauties. And a note, a note telling Audrey that he was very, very sorry, and that he wanted her to give him a chance to prove himself, to prove that he was a decent man who admired her and held her in high esteem....

No, that wouldn't work. She'd never accept that as the truth.

If it even *was* the truth. He wasn't certain he held her in high esteem. As much as it sickened him, he had to acknowledge that his feelings for Audrey had nothing to do with the high esteem in which he held her.

Audrey could see right through him. He might not understand her, but she understood him, better than he understood himself. She understood that when a man, even a decent, respectful man, saw a woman dressed tartily and flashing her feminine assests, deep-seated male longings were unleashed that had no relationship to esteem.

Brandon wanted to make love to Audrey. He wanted her. It was as simple as that.

Three

––––––

Audrey collapsed onto the swivel chair behind the desk in her windowless inner office at the university. Exhaustion overwhelmed her, weighing down on her shoulders like a thick leaden mass. She'd worked at the Angel Club only one weekend, and already she felt drained. She wondered how long she'd be able to stick it out.

She'd been well enough rested Sunday, having slept until noon. She'd gotten home especially late Saturday night—or early Sunday morning—having gone out for a cup of coffee with Iris after closing time. But then Sunday evening she'd arrived at the club to find flowers waiting for her. And she hadn't slept at all that night.

She didn't like flowers, at least not bouquets men sent to women. Her father was always giving flowers to her mother, symbols of penance for his many sins. It was easier for a man to treat a woman to flowers than to treat her with dignity, Audrey knew.

When she carried the three red roses Brandon had sent her to the dressing room, she'd been tempted to flush them down the toilet. But Iris and the other waitresses were there, and they'd made such a to-do about the beautiful blossoms that Audrey believed disposing of them would be an insult to her colleagues. So she'd jammed them into a tumbler of water from the kitchen and brought them home with her at the end of the night.

At home she again contemplated throwing them out, but something had prevented her. Maybe it was his note.

She pulled it out of her briefcase, unwilling to consider why she'd bothered bringing it to campus with her. Somehow she knew she'd want to read it again and again. She unfolded the thick cream-colored stationery and spread it before her on her desk, then forced her weary eyes to focus on Brandon's elegant script: *I don't blame you for thinking the worst of me, but first impressions can be false. Please call me and give me another chance.* Then he'd jotted down his telephone number and signed it, rather formally, "Brandon Q. Fox."

Q? Was it his middle initial that had intrigued her enough to save the note? Probably his middle name was Quincy. Or Quentin. There—mystery solved. She ought to just discard the note and be done with it.

But no, it wasn't just his middle initial that kept her from throwing away his note. It was his blunt assessment of himself. At least the man was honest about himself.

And his willingness to let her call him struck her as, well, not exactly macho. A *real* macho type would probably hang out at the Angel Club, badgering Audrey until she surrendered to his advances or until he gave up and set his sights on a new conquest. He wouldn't offer her the opportunity to make the next move. Brandon's willingness to supply her with his phone number and wait for her to take control indicated a small degree of respect for her on his part.

Or maybe it wasn't anything about his note that had compelled Audrey to save the flowers and to carry the neatly folded stationery with her. Maybe it was simply the man. Maybe it was the fact that, much as she hated to acknowledge it, she found him terribly attractive.

But why? Since she began to work at the Angel Club, he had visited not once but twice, which doubled his offensiveness in her eyes. What was more, the second time he'd visited, he'd had in tow another woman. A *married* woman, no less. Talk about indiscretion! Such actions certainly weren't the way to win Audrey's heart.

Yet Brandon couldn't possibly know the way to win Audrey's heart. As far as he knew, she was just another waitress in just another girlie joint. How could he know that the sort of man who could melt her heart had to be gentle, honest, moral, forthright...in short, the sort of man who probably didn't exist. Audrey had never met one of that species.

His note *was* forthright, she'd admit that much. Forthright and honest. It left no doubt in her mind that if she didn't phone him he'd never bother her again. He was leaving the decision up to her.

A light rap on her door jolted her from her ruminations, and she hastily stuffed the note back into her briefcase before calling out, "Come on in."

The door swung open and Liz Simpson bounded in. Liz taught composition courses in the English department, and she and Audrey had become friends soon after Audrey joined the faculty a year ago. "Greetings," the boisterous red-haired woman said as she walked across the tiny cubicle to Audrey's desk and plopped herself onto the molded plastic chair beside it. "Wanna sign a petition?"

"Which petition?" Audrey asked. It seemed as if at least once a week some petition or other was being circulated around the campus. And Liz was usually the chief organizer of the petitions.

Liz shoved a stapled wad of papers onto Audrey's desk. "It's kind of an *amicus curiae* thing about the class-action lawsuit some women are bringing against the Capital Club."

Audrey lifted her eyes to Liz. She had heard a little about the Capital Club, but since she'd lived in Albany only slightly more than a year, she wasn't exactly up on all of the city's social organizations. "What class-action suit?"

"The Capital Club," Liz patiently explained, "is a private men's club, about a hundred and fifty years old. Its members are businessmen, politicos, local artists, you name it—as long as they've got money and don't wear dresses. A group of businesswomen is bringing suit, charging sex discrimination."

"That sounds like my kind of petition," Audrey agreed with a chuckle. She skimmed the brief text of the petition, which stated succinctly that the undersigned supported the women in their suit and believed that organizations at which business was conducted, and which received state and federal tax abatements due to their nonprofit status, were required to open their doors to all qualified members, male or female. It also encouraged current members to resign from the club in protest until the club allowed women to join.

Audrey signed without hesitation. "Are they going to hit us up for money?" she asked.

Liz shook her head. "The plaintiffs are *business-*women," she emphasized. "They can afford it. Besides, I hear they're getting some funds from one of the national women's organizations and the A.C.L.U. All we profs are offering is moral support. We've even gotten a bunch of men to sign. And two deans have resigned their membership."

"Good for them," Audrey said enthusiastically as she handed the petition back to Liz.

Liz folded it and slipped it into her canvas tote bag, then directed her attention to Audrey. "You look pooped, Audrey. Aren't you eating your Wheaties?"

"I was too tired to eat breakfast," Audrey confessed.

"Then let's have lunch. Have you got some time?"

Audrey checked her watch and nodded. Her afternoon lecture didn't start until two o'clock, and as tired as she was, she was even hungrier. She zipped shut her briefcase and rose.

"It's drizzling out," Liz remarked as they left the office. "Let's take the underground route." The university's campus was a sprawling conglomeration of stark white buildings connected by an enormous concrete plaza above and by a maze of tunnels below. According to rumor, the complex had originally been designed for some Middle-Eastern sultanate, but when that nation had ultimately decided not to use the architectural design, the State University of New York purchased it for its new Albany campus. It wasn't exactly a bad design—though its striated glass-and-concrete buildings reminded Audrey of cages—but it showed great ignorance about upstate New York's chilly climate. The arrangement of the buildings created vicious wind tunnels, and by the time the air held the first hint of winter, most students and staff preferred to travel from one building to another via the basement tunnels.

"Tough class this morning?" Liz asked as they descended to the cellar and entered one of the gloomy subterranean corridors.

They had to flatten themselves against a wall as a maintenance man driving a forklift careered past them, and Audrey waited until they'd resumed walking before answering. "The usual," she allowed. "Margaret Mead and the Samoan aborigines."

"I should think Margaret Mead would be one of your idols," Liz commented on Audrey's glum tone.

"She is," Audrey said. "It just bothers me that my students seem to think anthropology is simply a study of primitive cultures half a world away. Whenever I remind them that Americans can also be subject to anthropological analysis, they assume I'm referring to Native Americans of the previous century. They refuse to recognize that they're as much a part of a culture as anyone else."

"The semester is yet young," Liz consoled her. "Don't give up. Maybe your aspirations are too high," she added. "If I can get my students to spell the word *the* by the end of the term, I consider myself a success."

They reached the building housing the faculty dining room and climbed the stairs to the second floor. A work-study student seated them, and they ordered salads and coffee. Audrey requested that her coffee be brought immediately, and as soon as the waitress had poured it she took a long, bracing gulp of the strong black brew, hoping it would keep her awake.

Liz scrutinized her thoughtfully. "You really look beat, Audrey. It can't just be the teaching that's got you wiped out. It's only Monday, for heaven's sake."

Audrey nodded. "I started my tour of duty at the Angel Club this past weekend," she revealed. She had discussed her book at length with Liz, and she had no reason to hide her research strategy from her colleagues on campus.

Liz leaned forward expectantly. "How did it go?"

"It's ghastly," Audrey confessed with a shudder. "I mean, my uniform...Liz, it's truly disgusting. It's so low-cut, I look like I'm about to fall out of the damned thing."

"You?" Liz asked in disbelief, her eyes focused on Audrey's diminutive bustline.

Audrey laughed. "I beef my bosom up with socks," she explained with a wave toward her chest. "One of the other waitresses suggested it. She said it brings bigger tips."

Liz wrinkled her nose, but her curiosity overruled her disapproval. "Is she right?"

"I have no basis for comparison, since I haven't tried waitressing as my flat-chested self. But I must say the tips are outrageously good."

"So? Are you getting any good data from the experience?"

Audrey remained silent as the waitress delivered their salads. She made a mental note to leave the girl—another work-study student—a generous tip. Then she addressed Liz's question. "I think it'll be useful—if I don't drop dead of fatigue. Saturday night after work I went to an all-night diner for coffee with one of the waitresses. I like her, Liz—she's a sharp lady."

"Then why is she working at a joint like that?"

"Money," Audrey replied simply. "As I said, the tips are incredible. Iris told me she tries to live on her salary alone and dumps all her tips into a money market fund. She isn't an air-headed bimbo, appearances to the contrary."

"Why doesn't she get a better job?"

"She doesn't have much education," Audrey related. "None of the waitresses do, as far as I've gathered. And how many good-paying jobs are there for women without adequate schooling? She told me her boyfriend wants her to quit the job but she won't. If she did, she'd have to earn less money doing something else, and then she'd be more dependent on him for things. I've got to admire her guts, Liz. She's definitely going to merit a few pages in my book."

Liz nibbled on her salad for several minutes, then asked, "How about the customers? What are they like?"

"Most of them are pretty sleazy," Audrey replied.

"Oh, yeah?" Liz's eyebrows arched. "Care to be specific?"

Audrey opened her mouth and then shut it. For some reason she was unable to tell Liz about Brandon Fox. Probably for the same reason she'd been unable to discard the roses he sent her. "Well," she hedged, "they like to put their arms around my waist and call me sweetie." Brandon hadn't done that, but his dinner companion the first night had.

"Yucch," Liz grunted.

"My opinion exactly," Audrey concurred.

When they were finished with their meals, she and Liz parted ways, Liz to collect more signatures on her petition and Audrey to review her lecture notes before her afternoon class. As she strolled alone through the underground tunnel back to her office, she tried to come to terms with her reluctance to tell Liz about Brandon. Why on earth did she feel compelled to protect him? He was no less despicable than any of the other men who came to the Angel Club.

But his note... *first impressions can be false.* Maybe it was just a line, but maybe it was the truth. Maybe he wasn't as much of a jerk as he'd seemed.

"Nah," she refuted herself with a sniff. Men had used lines on her before. They liked to present themselves as paragons of virtue as they endeavored to strip a woman of that self-same virtue. Brandon had made his intentions quite clear that first evening—and then he'd added insult to injury by showing up at the club the following night with another woman. Did he honestly expect Audrey to think highly of him after that?

On the other hand, he might be exactly like her first impression of him: a typical Angel Club patron. In which case, she could probably get some fantastic information for her book from him. She could learn firsthand what sort of man frequented girlie clubs—not just by collating an abstract profile of his tribal habits but by delving into him as an individual. Just as her chat with Iris had personalized Audrey's data about waitresses at such establishments, so a conversation or two with Brandon Fox could offer invaluable insights into the customers at such establishments.

Hands-on experience, she mused as she arrived at her office and slipped her folder of notes from her briefcase. *All in the name of research.* Telephoning Brandon Fox might not be the safest way to gain experience, but what a boon it would provide to her book! If she called him, and if she got a sense that she could meet with him on safe turf, in full view of witnesses the risk would be worth it, she decided.

She phoned him after dinner that evening. Standing in the kitchen of the compact house she owned not far from campus, she dialed the number he'd provided and stared at the roses, which she'd stuffed haphazardly into an empty mayonnaise jar. The blossoms' velvety crimson petals were just beginning to spread open, and as much as she distrusted the intent behind them, she couldn't deny their beauty. As soon as Brandon answered his phone she turned her back on the flowers so as not to be distracted. "Hello," he said.

"Fox? This is Audrey," she identified herself.

"Audrey!" He sounded uncommonly pleased that she'd phoned him. "Hello!"

Don't get your hopes up, buddy, she mumbled silently. "Look, Fox, what's the deal here?" The words were uncharacteristically harsh coming from her, but she wanted him to think of her only as a brassy Angel Club waitress. If he knew she was eager to dissect him for research purposes, he'd never agree to see her.

"There's no deal," he said calmly. "I only want you to forgive me for being so rude the other night."

"If I said I forgave you, would you say goodbye?" she challenged him.

He didn't immediately reply. "No," he finally confessed. "I'd like to see you."

"Why?"

"Why?" He faltered for a moment; apparently he hadn't thought things out that far. "Because I like your eyes," he said.

Well, she'd give him points for being forthright. "Let me set down the rules, Fox, and you see if you can live with them," she announced gruffly. "We go someplace public and well-lit. You don't touch me. You don't make any more nasty remarks about after-hours customers."

"Fine on all counts," he yielded.

That was quick, she mused. But of course he couldn't have said anything else. "All right, Fox. Meet me after work on Friday. I get off at one. Wait for me by the front door."

"I'll be there," he promised before hanging up.

The restaurant was fairly quiet Friday evening, the first day of the Columbus Day weekend. Evidently the Angel Club's customers felt it necessary to be dutiful husbands and fathers on a holiday. Although Audrey's back and legs were still cramped, she was reasonably awake and energetic as closing time rolled around.

In the dressing room she stripped off her uniform and pulled her street clothes from her locker. She tugged on her jeans and turtleneck sweater, then studied her reflection in the mirror. The sweater wasn't bulky enough to hide the puny dimensions of her breasts. Brandon would be sure to notice the sudden shrinkage in Audrey's figure, and that might make him suspicious. Sighing, she jammed her socks into the stretchy cups of her bra. Her boots, while not too comfortable when worn without socks, rose high on her calves beneath the legs of her jeans, so Brandon would never know that she was wearing her socks on the wrong appendages.

She washed off her makeup, ran her brush through the thick black shag of her hair and sighed again. *Research,* she reminded herself, trying to quell her apprehension about meeting him. She didn't think he'd make any more nasty remarks about whether she accepted men as customers outside the Angel Club, but she still didn't trust him. She hoped she wouldn't have to engage in a wrestling match with him. Especially since such a wrestling match would in all likelihood dislodge her socks from her bra.

Bidding the other waitresses farewell, she left the dressing room and ambled down the corridor to the restaurant's entry. As promised, Brandon was waiting there for her. He too wore jeans, and a cable-knit sweater of pale blue which hinted at the athletic contours of his chest. The sweater's color made his eyes appear more blue than gray.

Audrey made a concerted effort to ignore his overwhelming good looks.

"Hello," he murmured as she drew to a halt beside him. He seemed almost diffident, his voice subdued and his gaze focused on her face. Apparently he wasn't going to embarrass her by leering at her phony 38-D bustline.

"Okay, Fox," she declared crisply, determined to remain in Angel Club-Audrey character. "Here I am."

"Here you are," he agreed, his quiet tone reflecting his appreciation.

Unnerved by her body's instantaneous warming in his presence, she started toward the door. "There's a twenty-four-hour diner we can go to," she said, shoving the door open when Brandon made no move to hold it for her. The place she had in mind was the diner she'd gone to with Iris last week. It had been well-lit, the stools along the counter populated by policemen and truckers. It seemed like a particularly safe place for her to visit with Brandon.

"Whatever you say," he rapidly assented.

She drew to a halt by her bike, and he frowned. "Why don't we take my car?" he suggested.

She shook her head. "No way, José. You can follow me there." Having her bike at the diner would ensure that she could make a quick escape if she had to. She strapped on her helmet, fastened her knapsack to the small chrome rack behind the bike's seat and ignited the engine.

Brandon didn't seem pleased by the traveling arrangement, but he didn't argue with her. He crossed the lot to his Volvo and climbed in.

Riding to the diner, Audrey was sharply aware of the square silver sedan tailing her bike. Her body's reaction to Brandon when they'd met in the restaurant made her question the wisdom of her research tactic. As much as she despised Brandon, she couldn't deny the very real possibility that research had nothing to do with her decision to meet him after work. Simply by being a customer at the Angel Club he represented everything she abhorred about men, yet despite her animosity she couldn't resist the visceral attraction she felt toward him. Intellectually she detested the man, but her flesh warred with her intellect. Brandon Fox was a fox in more ways than one.

With a stern warning to keep her defenses up and to bear in mind her purpose in going out with him, she steered into the diner's parking lot and braked. Brandon parked and joined her as she dismounted from the bike. She pulled off her helmet as they climbed the cement stairs to the glass door and entered the glaringly lit diner.

A bleary-eyed waitress led them to a booth, and Audrey suffered a pang of empathy for the woman. It was bad enough having to work at such an exhausting job until one o'clock. She'd never be able to stomach a full night of waitressing.

After a quick perusal of the laminated menu, Audrey ordered a cup of coffee. Brandon requested hot chocolate, and the waitress took their menus and abandoned the table.

Audrey shrugged out of her denim jacket and laid it beside her helmet on the vinyl seat. Brandon watched her, his gentle eyes absorbing her every motion. "Why do you ride a motorcycle?" he asked.

"It's not a motorcycle," she told him. "It's a motorbike. One step removed from a moped." The waitress delivered their beverages, and Audrey warmed her hands on the steaming cup of coffee set before her. She'd have to start wearing gloves on the bike, she thought.

"Whatever it is," Brandon persisted, "it isn't the safest thing on the road, is it?"

"It's one of the cheapest things on the road," Audrey explained honestly. "The last car I owned was a lemon." She'd been in graduate school at the time, and when she had to dump the malfunctioning car she didn't have the funds to buy anything more expensive than her trusty motorbike.

"What do you do in the winter?" Brandon asked.

"I dress warmly."

He nodded and sipped his cocoa. Audrey observed the slender smoothness of his hands and recalled that he was probably a lawyer. His hands bore out that supposition. They clearly weren't hands that had been roughened by hard labor.

Audrey's eyes moved to his face. She had never performed a study of the faces of girlie-club patrons, but Brandon's didn't seem the right sort. There was an undefinable tenderness in his eyes and the pale laugh lines that framed them, an easy humor about his mouth, a candor in the way he returned her scrutiny. According to her studies, the behavior pattern of men like Brandon involved ogling women from a distance but being evasive when they encountered them up close. Indeed, they frequently found it easier to contemplate photographs of women in magazines than live women. They tended to be subliminally conscious that women didn't appreciate their leering, although among other men they believed that leering was a sign of their masculinity.

Brandon wasn't leering at Audrey. He was merely looking at her, concentrating on her eyes and then her lips. "You look so much prettier without all that makeup," he commented.

"The makeup's for work," she told him.

"I'd think you would want to look your prettiest at work," he hazarded.

"The men who come to the Angel Club want spicy, not pretty," Audrey muttered, adding silently, *I shouldn't have to tell you that, Fox.* "Let's not talk about me," she added. "Let's talk about you."

"What about me?" he asked innocently.

"What do you want with me?"

He mulled over his reply for several minutes, filling the time by drinking some of his cocoa. "Friendship?" he attempted.

Audrey laughed. "Right. And you also want to sell me the Brooklyn Bridge."

Brandon smiled, but his eyes retained their seriousness. "I'd like to get to know you better," he insisted.

"Why?" Audrey challenged him. If she could get a straightforward answer from him, it might prove quite useful to her book: sample man confesses the reason behind his attraction to girlie waitresses.

Brandon traced the rim of his cup with his finger. He flexed his mouth several times before speaking. "I'll be honest with you, Audrey—I don't know. You're not at all like the kind of women who usually interest me, but I find myself very attracted to you and I'm struggling to make sense of it."

That wasn't the answer she expected, and in fact it seemed rather useless to her. "What kind of women usually interest you?" she asked.

"Ambitious intellectuals," he freely admitted.

Audrey stifled a smirk. Maybe she *ought* to have expected such an answer. Brandon was trying to disguise his base male instincts by presenting himself as some cultured, proper gentleman—a paragon of virtue. Eager to goad him, she asked, "What makes you think I'm not an ambitious intellectual?"

"Working in a place like the Angel Club?" he count-ered. "If you were, you'd have a better job than that."

"It's a great job," she fibbed. "Terrific pay. And of course I get to meet all sorts of swell guys like you," she added sardonically.

"You've only been working at the Angel Club a week," he pointed out, ignoring her sarcastic tone. "What did you do before then?"

"I was a waitress," she told him. It wasn't a complete lie. "I worked at a place like this diner, out in Madison, Wisconsin. A college hangout type place."

"What brought you to Albany?"

Why was he asking all the questions? She tried to think of a way to turn the spotlight back on him, but she couldn't come up with any way to do so discreetly, so she answered, "Wanderlust, I guess."

"There must be college hangouts around the university here in town," he mentioned.

"College kids are lousy tippers," Audrey explained. "People who go to the Angel Club aren't. Your pal gave me a whopper of a tip last week."

"He's no pal of mine," Brandon grumbled, relieving Audrey of the need to direct the conversation toward him. "Actually, we're opponents, attorneys on opposite sides of a case."

"Were you trying out your arguments over dinner?"

Something flashed in his eyes, and Audrey briefly won-dered whether her question had sounded too...intellectual. If he didn't think Audrey was the ambitious, intellectual kind of woman he generally pursued, then any remotely intelligent comment on her part would probably take him by surprise. He cleared his throat before answering her. "We were discussing possible ways to avoid a trial. Prager suggested that we meet over dinner. I had no idea why he decided to take us to the Angel Club. I'd never been there before.''

"Sure, and you buy *Playboy* for the articles," she sniffed skeptically.

"I beg your pardon?"

She hid her grimace behind her coffee cup as she drank. Lowering it, she said, "You don't have to pretend you aren't a regular at the Angel Club. Face it, it's thanks to the regulars that I've got a job. So don't feel you've got to hand me some line about how you never set foot in the place before last Friday."

"But it's the truth," he defended himself.

"Uh-huh," she sniffed, a small grin teasing her lips. "Never been to the club, and then you show up twice in one weekend. Tell me about that bridge you want to sell me, Fox."

"Saturday night..." He paused to think, then declared, "I came back because I wanted to see you again."

"With your honey along for the ride?"

"Karen? She's not my 'honey.'" The word apparently didn't sit well with him, and he shifted uncomfortably in his seat. "She's just a friend of mine. I have lots of friends who are women."

"I'll bet," Audrey muttered cynically.

Brandon seemed driven to persuade her of his honorability. "Audrey, I'm not saying I don't...date women. I do."

"*Date* them?" She picked up on his euphemistic term.

"All right," he conceded. "I've known women as lovers, of course I have. But Karen isn't a lover, and she never has been. We work together; we're both associates at the same law firm. I'm good friends with her husband. He had to be out of town for the weekend, and I took her out to dinner so she wouldn't have to eat alone."

"Sure," Audrey sniffed. "The guy's back is turned for a weekend, so why not?"

"You're really determined to think the worst of me, aren't you," he retorted angrily.

"Well, what am I supposed to think? If you had only the noblest of motives, what the hell were you doing twice last weekend at the Angel Club? The food isn't *that* good. I know—I've eaten it. We waitresses get a free snack before opening time."

His tone was one of forced patience. "I went Friday night because it was a business dinner and the man who was hosting it took us there. I went Saturday night because Karen was curious to see the place."

"I thought you said you came because you wanted to see me," Audrey argued, feeling inexplicably disappointed.

"I *did*," Brandon maintained. "That was the only reason I let Karen talk me into going back." He fiddled with his teaspoon for a moment, then slammed it onto the table and pressed his palms against the surface, bearing down on Audrey. "Look. Let's not play games. I'm attracted to you. I'm intrigued by you. You're the only good thing about the Angel Club, as far as I could tell. I haven't stopped thinking about you. I was a bit clumsy, I put my foot in my mouth that first night, and I'm sorry. I'm grateful you agreed to see me after that. I'd like the opportunity to find out what could develop between you and me. There," he said, leaning back against the upholstery, his speech having drained him.

Audrey took a moment to digest his words. No question about it, the man was definitely forthright. He didn't seem to be fitting her researched profiles. But perhaps it was simply a matter of his being glib when it came to speech; he was an attorney, after all, a professional in the field of arguments and defenses.

Or maybe she was struck by his words because she was as attracted to him as he was to her, and as curious. His soft yet intense eyes intrigued her, his thick blond hair, his broad shoulders and lean body. In a way, she was as guilty as he was for being taken by appearances. If Brandon Fox had been attracted to the way Audrey's sexy uniform displayed her body, well, she was attracted to the way his sweater hugged his chest and his jeans clung to his long legs. He was without a doubt the sexiest-looking man she'd met in a long while.

She ought to have been bothered that what he was turned on by was a pair of rolled-up socks. She ought to have been even more bothered that she was guilty of doing what she condemned men for doing: being attracted to someone because of his appearance instead of his mind. Yet if Brandon was telling the truth—a big if, of course— he wasn't as shallow and superficial as she'd assumed him to be. What had he written in his note? *First impressions can be false.*

"Well?" he urged her. "I've bared my soul, Audrey. Say something."

"Bared your soul?" she said with a nervous laugh. She needed to cling to her first impression of him; it was her only defense against the sexual magnetism he emanated. "Do you think you're the first man who's ever been interested in an 'angel' at the Angel Club?"

"No," he allowed. "But for me it's a first."

"And what am I supposed to do about it? Humor you?"

"Give me a chance," he replied earnestly.

A chance at what? she wondered anxiously. A chance to find out whether her bra was padded with inorganic material? A chance to find out whether her temptress image at the club could be matched in performance? "If you're looking to experiment on me, Fox, forget it," she murmured. "I wasn't put on earth just to give you your jollies. I know most men believe that's what women are for, but—"

"But I'm not one of them," he asserted quietly but firmly. "I'm not looking for 'jollies.'"

"What are you looking for?" she pressed him.

His gaze wandered slowly over her face, then dropped to her small hands where they rested on the table beside her empty coffee cup. "I'm looking for you," he whispered. "I'm looking to find out who you are, why I'm haunted by you, why I can't stop thinking about you. I'm looking to make sense of this whole thing. I'm looking—I'm looking to be your friend. I know, I know," he quarreled with himself. "That sounds almost as unbelievable as what I said by the men's room last week. Audrey, I'm usually good at expressing myself, but you do things to me and I just don't know how to put them into words. I'm trying. At least you've got to give me credit for trying."

If he were someone else, she'd expect him to launch into a monologue about how his wife didn't understand him, about how he was just a mixed-up fellow who needed the love of a pretty woman to save him, about how a night spent in Audrey's arms would solve all his problems. She knew the lines. But Brandon seemed to be struggling so deeply with himself that she couldn't take his statement as a string of lies designed to seduce her. She ought to, but she couldn't. "A friend," she echoed. "I don't know, Brandon."

Her use of his first name startled and pleased him. His eyes brightened slightly, and the corners of his lips twitched upward. "You don't have to know," he remarked gently. "All you have to do is give me a chance."

"Well..." Was he truly asking the impossible? If she gave him a chance, if she allowed him to become her friend, the absolute worst that could happen would be that she'd garner some interesting information for her book. The best that could happen would be that she'd have a new friend. "A chance," she yielded, keeping her tone as emotionless as possible. "What the heck. I'm a gambler."

"You've got to be, to risk your life on the roads riding that motorcycle of yours," he said. Audrey checked the impulse to correct his calling her bike a motorcycle. He was already signaling the waitress for a check. As she approached, he dug into his hip pocket for his wallet and pulled out a dollar bill.

"Give her a bigger tip," Audrey ordered him. "It's tough being a waitress."

He smiled wryly and handed the waitress a second dollar. Then he stood. "It's late," he noted. "You must be tired."

"Wiped out," she confirmed, slinging on her jacket and scooping her helmet off the seat.

They walked together to the door, and this time Brandon held it open for her. The night had grown even chillier while they'd been inside the diner, and the frigid air numbed Audrey's fingers. She'd have to start wearing gloves, she reminded herself again.

Brandon accompanied her to her motorbike, and she lifted her helmet to strap onto her head. He stopped her, pulling the helmet from her hands and balancing it on the seat. "When can I see you again?" he asked.

"I...don't know."

"Tomorrow?"

"No," she said. "I've got a lot to do tomorrow." It was the truth; she had to start inserting her Angel Club impressions into her manuscript.

"Sunday, then?"

"I work, you know," she pointed out. "Thursday through Sunday nights till one."

"During the day. If it's nice we could have a picnic."

A picnic? Audrey pictured her fingertips turning blue from the cold and wondered why in the world Brandon would suggest such an idea. During the day, of course, it would be warmer. Maybe an invitation to a picnic was his way of proving that she'd be safe in his company. An *alfresco* lunch in broad daylight wouldn't provide the privacy he'd need to seduce her. "I tell you what," she conceded. "Give me a call Sunday morning. Late," she stressed. "I sleep late."

He nodded, then pulled out his wallet again and located a business card inside it. He groped in his other hip pocket and produced a pen. "I need your number," he said. Audrey recited it, and he wrote it down.

They stood for several silent moments in the lot, the only light an eerie orange glow from a mercury street lamp on the corner. Then Brandon reached up and wove his fingers into the dense black curls of Audrey's hair. She watched as his face neared hers, as his lips moved to her mouth, and her mind went blank. No thoughts of research, of Brandon's two visits to the Angel Club, or the danger of losing her objectivity about him. Maybe Brandon liked intellectual women, but right now he would surely be delighted to know that Audrey's intellect had fled her, leaving in its wake a sensuous warmth that softened her body, readying it for his kiss.

Four

One of the ground rules was that he wasn't to touch her. But she didn't recoil from him as his mouth came down on hers. His kiss was hesitant, giving her the opportunity to retreat if she chose to. She didn't. Her lips felt soft and pliant as they molded themselves to his. He experienced a rush of heat through his body, and his hand tightened in her hair.

Brandon had kissed women before, but never a woman like Audrey. Never before had he felt such an immeasurable physical attraction that was so resistant to logic, so compelling. His mouth moved against hers, increasing in pressure. Still she made no attempt to withdraw from him.

His lips parted, and so did hers. He let his tongue venture along the full width of her lower lip, teasing its tender flesh, tasting her breath. Then he explored her teeth, and they parted as well.

When his tongue found hers, his mouth exploded from the intoxicating flavor of rich coffee mingling with sweet chocolate. He folded his other arm about her, sliding his hand beneath her jacket and flattening his palm against her narrow waist. She moaned, an exciting sigh of assent.

Another fiery gust tore through him, rising up from his loins to his brain, informing him that Audrey wanted him as much as he wanted her. It had never been like this before, he realized, never this sudden, this urgent. He wanted her in a way he'd never wanted any other woman.

If he ever returned to rationality, he'd probably be disappointed in himself for reveling in such strong, imperative feelings for a woman like Audrey. She seemed to have none of the characteristics he'd always considered important in a woman: education, professional stature, a cultured, intellectual approach to the world. Audrey wasn't anything like that. What was she? A cheap waitress who rode a motorcycle and boasted large breasts. Those weren't the sorts of traits that meant much to Brandon.

Except that right now they did. Right now his body fought against rationality and demanded that he simply accept Audrey for what she was and respond as he was responding.

His hand slid down to the curve of her bottom, forcing her hips to his. She moaned again.

"I want you," he breathed, breaking the kiss.

"Obviously," she murmured, her hips arching reflexively against him.

"You want me too," he said softly.

"Brandon..." She struggled for breath. "I don't know, I—"

He recognized that she intended to refuse him, so he cut off her words with another kiss. Her voice melted into a groan, and he dug his fingers into the dense black waves of her hair, reaching down to her neck and caressing it with his thumb.

Her hands slid up to his shoulders. Their grip was strong despite their slender delicacy, and Brandon wanted to believe that it was her desire alone which made her cling so insistently to him. His hips swayed against hers, and her arms tightened around him as her body matched his movements.

His tongue filled her mouth again, dazzled by the enticing dampness, the eager motion of her tongue against his. His fingers worked beneath the ribbed edge of her sweater to stroke the smooth, warm skin of her back. He felt crazy with longing, and he didn't care.

He traced the ridge of her spine as high as her bra strap, then wandered forward along her ribs. Just before he reached the underside of her breast she drew back abruptly. "Don't," she whispered shakily.

His hold on her loosened slightly, his hand dropping away from her body. His gaze sharpened on her averted face, and he noticed her lowered eyes and her flushed cheeks. She hadn't objected to his touching her hips, her buttocks, to the sensual rhythm of his thighs against hers. But her breasts—clearly he'd pushed his luck. She wouldn't let his exploration extend to them.

He found such sudden inhibition on her part bizarre. At the Angel Club, she marched around all but naked, her full bosom practically bursting out of her skimpy uniform. Evidently she didn't mind displaying her breasts, but she wouldn't permit him to touch them.

He didn't dare to question her, however. He'd already overstepped the boundaries she'd laid out for him. He should consider himself fortunate that she hadn't slapped him or kicked him.

"I want you," he repeated quietly. "We want each other. There's nothing to be ashamed of."

"I'm not ashamed," she mumbled, righting her sweater and buttoning the denim jacket protectively around her torso.

"But—?"

"But nothing. I'm not ready for this, Fox. You're—you're rushing me."

He felt an unexpected twinge of anger. It wasn't as if she were a blushing virgin, for crying out loud! If she was, she wouldn't be working in a place like the Angel Club, exposing her body for all to see.

But he controlled his rage. Her job shouldn't lead him to the wrong conclusions. Maybe she'd been honest when she said she worked at the club simply because the tips were good. He reminded himself that not all women had the opportunity to get a good education and work at a dignified job. He shouldn't judge her by her revealing waitressing uniform, and he shouldn't rush her only because his body was rushing him.

His muscles still taut with the need for her, he lifted her helmet from the seat of her motorcycle and handed it to her. "I'll phone you Sunday morning," he said before pivoting on his heel and forcing himself to leave her.

"Late," she called after him.

He drove home in a blur of emotion. None of this made sense. He'd hoped that meeting with her again would bring his feelings into alignment, but if anything, they seemed more tangled than before. He wanted Audrey fiercely; his body blazed with an adamant yearning that all his rationalizing couldn't contain.

Not until he was in his apartment did it occur to him that his reaction to her might be rather typical. How many other men who saw her at the Angel Club wanted her?

Only a blind man or a homosexual *wouldn't* want her, he realized, and the thought spurred a surprising jealousy within him. Not only did he want Audrey, but he wanted her all to himself.

Don't rush her, he reprimanded himself as he stalked down the hall to his bedroom. Without bothering to undress, he sprawled out on his bed and closed his eyes. He couldn't rush her. He would have to hold back, to take things at her pace. Perhaps in time he could enlighten her to the world, influence her to leave the Angel Club, to seek a better life for herself. He could give her a stronger sense of her own value as a woman, her dignity as a human being. He could save her.

A self-deprecating laugh escaped him, and he opened his eyes again. He surveyed the well-appointed bedroom with its cream-colored walls, its sleek oak furnishings, the leather easy chair in one corner and the plush Persian rug covering the hardwood floor. He tried to picture Audrey in his room, lounging in the chair, perhaps, dressed in...no, he couldn't imagine her in pajamas, in a stodgy woolen robe. He could imagine her only in something silky and slinky, trimmed with sheer lace.

His imagination disappointed him. He wanted to respect Audrey. She deserved his respect as much as any other woman did.

He tried to view the world through her eyes. Seeing things from the point of view of his adversaries was a talent Brandon held in abundance. In his work it frequently enabled him to negotiate with the other side, to reach a compromise without having to drag a case through the courts and to save his clients time and money. Whenever he could, he tried to approach his clients' contentions from the perspective of their opponents in order to understand their positions and counter them effectively.

Audrey wasn't his opponent or his adversary—at least he hoped she wasn't. Still, he ought to try to put himself inside her head. Rather than imagining her in his room, he ought to imagine himself in hers.

What would her home look like? Probably a cramped apartment. She obviously didn't have much money; she said she'd taken the Angel Club job for the big tips. He pictured her in an efficiency apartment furnished with castoffs. A photograph of her parents in a frame on a shelf, perhaps, and a few personal knicknacks, a porcelain statuette of a Siamese cat, a cut-glass paperweight, a wicker basket to hold her mail. And a vase containing the roses Brandon had sent her.

Maybe there was a photograph of another man. It was possible. In fact, it was likely. She hadn't left Wisconsin because of wanderlust—she didn't seem like the roving type. She must have left for another reason. A relationship had disintegrated. A man had broken her heart. She had run away to lick her wounds. Why not?

To lick her wounds, and to wait for the man to come to his senses and beg her to return. Brandon could merely be someone with whom to pass the time until her Wisconsin lover crawled back to her on his knees....

"Damn," he grunted. Usually so calm, so sensible, he was allowing Audrey to turn him into an inventor of wild tales. What had she called him? A little boy with fantasies.

He forced himself to empty his mind as he heaved himself from the bed and moved to the bathroom to wash. He saw no point in concocting stories about her. If he approached her the way he usually approached women, he would simply take his time, get to know her and learn about her as their relationship progressed. That was how it should be. He would see her Sunday, in broad daylight.

They would eat and talk. Maybe he would learn whether some fellow was waiting for her back in Wisconsin.

As his physical frustration subsided he found himself looking forward to their Sunday date with cheerful anticipation. He *did* want to get to know her, at least as much as he wanted to make love to her. In many ways she seemed alien to him, but he knew that if he remained patient and open to her, he would learn a lot from her.

On Saturday he rose early, took a short jog through the drizzly morning and returned home to dry off. The day was raw and gray, perfect for baking bread. While he kneaded his dough he tried to guess how Audrey might spend her Saturdays. Sleeping late, he didn't doubt. Sleeping late, then eating a light breakfast, then running errands. No, she'd told him she worked Thursdays through Sundays. That left her her three weekdays during which she could shop, do her laundry, clean her apartment. Maybe on Saturdays she read. She curled up with a good book and lost herself in its pages. He wanted to believe that.

Once his dough was in the oven, he retired to his office-den to study his Capital Club file. A court date had been set, but Prager was eager to avoid a trial. Yet he wasn't eager enough to surrender to the twentieth century and persuade the club of its indefensible position. Brandon's clients weren't at all afraid of facing the club in court. Money was no obstacle, they claimed. They wanted to bring the Capital Club to its knees. Brandon didn't blame them.

Saturday evening he dined at home in solitude. Although he wasn't the sort to go into a panic when he found himself alone on a weekend night, such an occurrence was a rarity. He had a wide circle of female friends with whom he socialized. Yet during the week he'd felt no compulsion to call one up and invite her to join him for dinner. For some reason all his energy had been directed toward his Friday night meeting with Audrey. Even devouring an omelet in front of his television set didn't make him lonely. He didn't really want to see anyone else. He'd been with Audrey last night, and he'd be with her tomorrow. That was enough to satisfy him.

He awoke typically early on Sunday. He refrained from telephoning Audrey right away, although that was what he wanted to do. Her job must be truly exhausting, and so he kept himself occupied with another run, enjoying the return of the autumn sunshine after the previous day's gloomy rain. He stopped at a bakery for croissants before returning home, where he took a long, energizing shower and then breakfasted on his croissants and fresh fruit. By ten thirty his patience began to wear thin, and he pulled out the card on which he'd jotted Audrey's number and dialed it.

Her groggy voice when she answered informed him that he hadn't waited long enough. "Hullo?" she mumbled.

"I woke you up," he murmured contritely. "I'm sorry."

"Fox?" she said more clearly. "No...that's all right. I'm up."

That she was willing to lie to spare his feelings flattered him. "Are we on for today?" he asked.

"Hmm," she grunted, struggling for lucidity. "Picnic, right?"

"That's right. I'm glad we decided on today; yesterday would have been a washout."

"It's still going to be wet everywhere," she remarked.

"We'll go someplace dry. How about it? I've got a loaf of fresh-baked bread, a jug of wine...all I need is thou."

She laughed sleepily. "Spare me, Fox. I'm not susceptible to lines."

Susceptible. It wasn't the first time she'd offered a glimmer of erudition. Of course even high-school dropouts knew the word *susceptible,* but Brandon clung to each hint of Audrey's intelligence as if it were a precious gift. He wanted to believe she was smart, even though he knew she couldn't have had much education. "No lines," he responded to her jibe. "Just the truth, Audrey. When can I pick you up?"

She didn't answer right away. He visualized her glancing at her alarm clock, twisting in bed, her dark, lush hair splayed across the pillow. *Dangerous thoughts,* he chastised himself. If he kept thinking that way he'd be tempted to attack her the moment he saw her. He couldn't rush her. He had to keep his passion for her in check until she was ready for him.

"How about noon?" she suggested. "I need to get some coffee down my throat."

"Noon it is. Where do you live?"

She gave him her address. He was amazed to learn that she lived in the same neighborhood as Karen and Tim. It wasn't an affluent neighborhood, but it was a charming residential area of neat houses. He wouldn't have expected Audrey to live in a house, especially since she'd arrived in Albany so recently.

But he concealed his surprise and assured her that he knew the general area. She told him her house was small with brown shingles, and he promised to call for her at twelve.

He dressed in clean jeans and a tan oxford shirt. Audrey had worn jeans and a sweater Friday after work, and he suspected that her street clothes offered a strong indication of her tastes. She'd worn boots, too—Brandon supposed boots were necessary when one rode a motorcycle—and an almost hippielike dungaree jacket.

The only boots he owned were rugged leather hiking shoes, which he hadn't cleaned the mud from since the summer, when he'd spent a vacation week backpacking in the Adirondacks. He decided on sneakers instead, and a brown crew-neck sweater in case the afternoon grew cool.

He packed a paper bag with the loaf of bread he'd baked the previous day, as well as a wedge of Jarlsburg cheese, a paring knife, a chilled bottle of Riesling, two plastic glasses and a corkscrew. Audrey was correct in her assessment that the ground would be too soggy to picnic on, so he didn't bother bringing a blanket. He decided that they'd have their picnic at the state university campus. Its broad paved mall, stretching among the classroom and office buildings, was decorated with a huge fountain and several small garden groves lined with benches. It would be a lovely place to take Audrey. Maybe she'd enjoy being surrounded by academic buildings. Maybe he'd convince her to go back to school, to make more of her life than she could ever hope to accomplish at the Angel Club.

He arrived at her house a few minutes early. The house was tidy, the front lawn recently mowed and edged, the shrubs carefully pruned. Her motorcycle was parked in the driveway before the garage. He parked beside the bike and strolled up the slate walk to the door.

She answered his ring almost at once and joined him outside on the front step, slamming the door shut behind herself. It dawned on Brandon that she didn't want to allow him into her house. Was she afraid that he'd take advantage of her the minute he crossed the threshold? Well, such a fear was probably justified, he granted as he recalled the flame of desire that had ignited between them the last time they'd been alone together.

In the bright midday light she looked even more beautiful to him. She wore no makeup at all, yet her eyes seemed astonishingly large and dark, her lashes long and delectably curly. Her lips were a soft pink color, her cheeks a healthy rosy hue. Her faded jeans were snug along her slender legs, and her tweedy cowl-neck sweater played down her voluptuous breasts. "Hello, Fox," she greeted him.

"Hello." He considered kissing her cheek, but decided not to. While she didn't appear unfriendly, she had warned him not to rush her, and he wanted to prove his respectability to her.

"Did you think of a dry place for a picnic?" she asked.

He nodded. "The Podium."

"Huh?"

"The state university campus. It's just down the road from here. It has a huge promenade called the Podium, with lots of trees and a fountain."

"I don't want to go there," she said rapidly.

"Why not? It's really lovely there."

She bit her lower lip and shook her head.

Brandon wondered why she had such a strong aversion to the campus. Having lived in Albany so short a time, she'd probably never even seen the place. "Come on," he said, urging her down the front walk. "You'll like it. It's very nice."

Despite her reluctance, she didn't resist his suggestion further until they reached his car. "I don't know, Fox," she muttered. "A campus? Do we have to?"

"It doesn't look like a campus," he told her. "It looks like—an arts complex. I spend a lot of time there, using the school's library." He groped for a stronger argument; he honestly wanted to show her what a fine place the university was. As an Albany resident, she could attend classes inexpensively. She ought to learn about the resources available to her. "Consider, Audrey—it's an open-air public place. What could be safer?"

That seemed to persuade her. "All right," she relented.

"I tell you what," he offered, feeling obliged to make amends with her, though he wasn't sure why. "It's so close by, we can take your motorcycle."

Her eyes flashed, dark and mysteriously profound. "Do you want to?"

"I've never ridden on one of these things before," he said, inspecting her bike. "It must be fun."

She shrugged. "Okay," she agreed. "Hop on."

The seat was short, and he had to press up close to her to keep from falling off backward. She didn't bother to fetch helmets, and he didn't mention them to her. The university was only a few blocks away.

She revved the engine, then backed carefully past his car to the street. "Hang on," she warned him before shifting into first gear.

He clung to their picnic bag with one hand, resting the parcel on his thigh, and wrapped his other arm tightly around her waist. As the bike lurched forward her hair whipped back into his face. It smelled clean and woodsy; obviously she had recently washed it with an herbal shampoo.

The vibrations of the bike beneath them were oddly stimulating. So was the warmth of Audrey's back as she leaned into Brandon. His hand brushed the buckle of her leather belt, and her shoulders shifted, rubbing against his chest. Maybe this wasn't such a good idea after all, he mused as he tried to retain his equilibrium.

That she knew the way to the university campus pleased him. Once she steered into the main entry off Washington Avenue, he directed her to a visitors' parking lot and she parked. He was relieved to be off the bike, to put some distance between her and himself until he got his longing for her under control again.

She waited for him to lead the way, and he followed a path cutting across a stretch of grass to a stairway which rose to the mezzanine. An evenly planted copse of small pine trees stood in a recess among a group of buildings, and Brandon ushered Audrey to one of the vacant benches. The campus was relatively empty at this end. The opposite end of the plaza contained the library, and that was probably the only academic building that attracted students in large numbers on Sunday.

They settled on the bench, the paper bag between them. "You knew where the campus was," Brandon observed in a casual voice as he pulled the wine from the bag.

"Uh-huh," she mumbled vaguely, then laughed. "I live so close by, why shouldn't I know where it is?"

He applied the cockscrew to the bottle, again keeping his tone light when he asked, "Did you go to college?"

She turned to stare at the aromatic pines and ran her fingers thoughtfully through her hair, combing out its windswept tangles. "Yeah," she answered. "Out in Wisconsin."

He eyed her, then removed the glasses from the bag. "With a college degree," he commented, trying not to sound too condemning, "can't you find better work than waitressing?"

She eyed him, then scowled. "You don't think waitressing is good enough for me?"

He hesitated before pouring the wine. He tried to interpret her frown, which was contradicted by the upward tilt of her lips. "I think there are jobs that might be less of a strain on you, with bigger salaries."

"For instance, taking on male customers after hours?" she goaded.

He cringed. "You're never going to forgive me for saying that, are you," he muttered.

She laughed, and once he poured the wine she accepted a glass from him. "Anyway, I don't have a degree," she revealed. "I never finished."

He nodded. Things began to fall sensibly into place. She was bright, she spoke well. But for some reason she hadn't been able to obtain a diploma, so she was forced to find work where she could—at a sleazy place like the Angel Club if that was the only job available.

"How about you?" she asked. "Where'd you go to school?"

"Brown University," he replied softly.

"And law school?"

"Columbia," he said, muffling his tone even more.

But not enough. She heard him clearly, and she issued a hoot. "Hoity-toity, aren't you? Brown and Columbia? I'm surprised you don't have ivy growing up your legs."

Her attitude struck him as more mocking than joking, and he cringed again. He was afraid his pedigreed education would overwhelm her, perhaps make her feel insecure or inferior. That was the last thing he wanted, and he hastily reassured her by stating, "It isn't like that. I mean, I...had some opportunities and I took advantage of them. I was lucky."

"And I wasn't?" she challenged him. "Is that what you're saying?"

She seemed to have gone beyond mocking. There was a definite bitterness in her manner, a defensiveness that he longed to overcome. "What I'm saying," he said evenly, "is that I was lucky to be able to get that sort of education. I'm lucky to be working at a job because I enjoy it, not because it pays good tips."

"You," Audrey bluntly declared, "are patronizing me."

Again he was struck by her vocabulary, and by her astute perception. He studied her face, the stern line of her lips, and he fleetingly recalled the way they'd felt against his own. He chased the memory away with a brisk shake of his head. "Audrey," he claimed, "if I sound patronizing, I'm sorry. I'm only saying that you seem to have so much on the ball—I can't understand why you're willing to put on that tawdry uniform and work in a tawdry restaurant."

She reflected for a moment, then smiled wryly. "Maybe I figure it's a good way to pick up a rich lawyer."

Her tone and her expression puzzled him. He wasn't sure what she was driving at. "I'm not rich," he disputed her.

She threw back her head and laughed again. He loved the melifluous sound of her laughter. "Oh, come on, Fox," she protested. "Brown and Columbia, and now you're a lawyer. I know your type."

"I don't think you do," he argued steadily. "I'm not a fat-cat lawyer. I earn a comfortable living, but I'm not in law for the money."

"What are you in it for?"

Despite the taunting quality of her voice, she seemed genuinely interested. He sliced several pieces of cheese, then tore off two chunks of bread and handed one to her. "This may sound corny, but I'm in it for justice. I practice civil rights law, an occasional environmental case but mostly civil rights."

"Such lofty principles," she teased before biting into the bread. "Then you get down from your pedestal and spend your evenings at the Angel Club." She chewed and swallowed. "This bread is delicious," she commented.

He wanted to question her cynicism, her obvious bitterness about him—or about patrons of the Angel Club. But he decided it was safer to say, "Thank you. I baked it myself."

"You did?" She chuckled. "I supposed you slaved over a hot stove for hours."

"I really did," he snapped, her contemptuousness cracking his patience. "I bake bread every week. Why the hell do you have so little difficulty thinking the worst of me?"

His flaring anger seemed to startle her. Her disdainful smile faded, and she turned back to the trees and studied them for a long moment. "I'd like to think the worst of you, Brandon," she murmured. "But I'm having difficulty."

Her tone, and her use of his first name, convinced him that she was telling the truth. "Why do you want to think the worst of me?" he asked gently.

"Because you're—you're only interested in me for one thing, Fox," she said more forcefully. "You're a man. You're all after the same thing. You may talk a better line than most men, but when it comes to women, civil rights are something you leave in the office at five o'clock. It looks great on paper, but when you get right down to it, a pair of big breasts are really all you want in your women."

"No." His voice was quiet but vehement. "No, Audrey. I admit my initial attraction to you was physical. But I wouldn't keep coming back if that was all there was." She glanced skeptically at him. "What made you so bitter about men?" he asked.

She was spared from answering by the approach of a young man along the plaza. He spotted Audrey and waved. "Hey, Audrey!" he boomed.

Her cheeks darkened with a deep flush, and she shot the young man a quick, hard smile and a wave before turning away. The man evidently read her unwillingness to chat with him, because he nodded and walked past her and Brandon in the direction of the parking lot.

Brandon's eyes traced the young man, then settled on Audrey. Who was he? How did he know her? "A friend of yours?" Brandon inquired.

She pressed her lips together, then shrugged. "A classmate," she replied. "I'm...taking a couple of courses."

"You are?" Brandon's delight at this news illuminated his eyes. "That's wonderful! What are you taking?"

"Courses," she mumbled. She sipped her wine before elaborating, "A few here and there, maybe I can pull it together and get a degree."

"Fantastic!" Brandon squeezed her shoulder enthusiastically, but stifled the impulse to kiss her. "I knew it, Audrey, I knew you were too good for the Angel Club. You're too smart to tolerate that sort of work for long. You can get your degree and move on to something better. That's fantastic."

"You're a snob," she retorted. "It just so happens that most of the women who work at the Angel Club are too good for it. They're smart and savvy, and the only reason they work there is because men like you keep the place in business. Oh, sure, you're all so noble, in favor of civil rights and the whole thing, but then when it's time to unwind, you race to the nearest flesh joint to ogle and leer and nudge each other in the ribs. I know all about it, Fox."

Her scathing rage stunned him, and he took a few seconds to sort his thoughts. "What do you know about it?" he asked.

She said nothing.

"Audrey..." He sighed. "Whoever hurt you in the past, it wasn't me. I would never hurt you." His words took him by surprise, but as soon as he voiced them he knew they were the truth. "I wouldn't ever hurt you. I don't like the

Angel Club any more than you do. That's why I'm glad you're getting an education. I want you out of there.''

"So I'll be good enough for you?" she snorted.

"So...so you'll be good enough for yourself. I'm not the one who makes you feel belittled by your work. You feel it inside yourself. You're eager to defend how you earn your money, but I know you don't like it. We're really in agreement about this.''

"What, do you think getting a college diploma will automatically turn me into a madonna?" she scoffed. "Admit it, Fox, you don't want a madonna. If you did, you wouldn't have been attracted to me in the first place. You want an educated tart so you can continue to feel righteous while you gawk at my breasts.''

"What are you talking about, a madonna?''

"That's the way it is, isn't it?" she railed. "Two kinds of women: madonnas and whores. That's how men see it.''

"Where in the world did you ever pick up that notion?" he questioned her, his brow creasing in a stern frown.

"I was raised with it, Fox," she retorted. "It was bred into me by one of the best: my noble, righteous father. A fine, upstanding man, a pillar of the community, with schooling as fancy as yours. In theory as liberated as they come. But in practice...''

"In practice?''

A ragged sigh escaped her and she lowered her eyes to her lap. "In practice, show him a woman with cleavage and he turns into a slobbering idiot. In other words, a man, Fox. That's where I picked up my notions. And experience has only borne them out.''

The bitterness of her words caused his mind to reel. "Audrey," he whispered, tenderly brushing a curling tendril from her cheek. "Audrey, it isn't always like that. If you want respect as a woman, you ought to show some respect for men. We can't be categorized any more easily than women can.''

She lifted her eyes to his, and he found reason for hope in their striking clarity. She appeared almost rueful to him, wrestling with her doubt, struggling to believe him. ''You really just want to be my friend?'' she asked tremulously.

''Your friend, yes,'' he promised.

''*Just* my friend?''

He smiled wistfully. ''I'm a grown man, Audrey. I'd be lying if I said I wouldn't like to make love to you. But I'm not telling you anything you don't already know. You're a bewitchingly beautiful woman and I want you. After Friday night I'm sure you want me too. But if you're unwilling to follow through on that, I can bear it. I'd still want you as a friend.''

Unable to confront his candid confession, she dropped her gaze to the bread and helped herself to another chunk. ''You really baked this, huh?''

His smile expanded. He'd accept her reticence for now. He couldn't expect her to match him in frankness. Whatever wounds her past had inflicted on her made it difficult for her to deal with his honesty. If only she could believe that he wasn't like her father and the other men she'd known, he'd be content. It would be a minor victory, but he could live with it for now.

''Well,'' she said, emptying her glass. ''I've got some things to do this afternoon, and I've got to be at the club by four.''

He dutifully packed up the remains of their picnic. Obviously Audrey needed to be alone, to assess what Brandon had told her and to work through her feelings. Once more he reminded himself that he mustn't rush her. She seemed more receptive to him now than she had an hour ago, or two days ago. One small step at a time.

They left the grove for the parking lot and climbed onto the bike. As before, Audrey leaned comfortably back against him as she shifted into gear and guided the bike to the street. He let his hand drift over her abdomen, and she made no move to stop him.

She felt so good, her belly smooth and flat beneath his hand. Except for her breasts she had the lean, slender build he found most attractive on women. And she certainly couldn't control the size of her breasts. They were a genetic fact. The more time he spent with her, looking at her, admiring her, the more appealing he found her buxom figure.

They stopped at a red light, and once it changed the bike jolted forward. His balance shifted slightly, and his hand slipped upward as he tried to hold himself on the seat. Audrey forcefully batted his hand back down.

Maybe she was self-conscious about her breasts, he mused. Maybe her miserable experience included a number of men who had groped her or made crude remarks. Maybe she'd physically developed at a young age and suffered the indignities of her male classmates trying to cop feels from her in the school hallways. He wasn't so old that he couldn't recall the cruelty of teenage boys.

They arrived at her house and she coasted up the driveway, braking next to his car. Climbing off the bike, she said, "Thanks for the picnic, Fox. I've really got to run."

He grasped her arm and prevented her from leaving him. When he bowed to kiss her, she made no move to escape. His arms tightened around her, and he let his lips dance over her chin, her cheeks, her brow. She shivered slightly, her arms coiled about his waist, her mouth discovering the warm hollow beneath his chin.

"Let me come inside," he pleaded softly.

She nestled her head against his shoulder and sighed. "No."

"Are you afraid of me?"

"No."

"Then what? I'm rushing you?"

She sighed again, a hoarse, throaty breath. "Yes."

"Tell me what you want," he requested, his own voice rough and thick. "We're two mature people, Audrey, two adults with something pretty exciting happening between us. Tell me what you want to do about it."

"I want to think," she begged him weakly. "You said I'm smart. I'm smart enough to know I need some time to think."

"How long?" he asked, then chuckled. "I'm sorry. You do things to my self-control, woman. Especially when you kiss me that way," he added as her mouth softly touched his throat.

"*I'm* sorry," she murmured, drawing back, her lids lowered and her hands falling from his sides.

"Don't ever be," he chided her. "I love what you do to me, even if it drives me crazy."

"I don't mean to drive you crazy," she apologized.

His eyes narrowed on her downcast face. "Do you mean to drive yourself crazy?" he asked.

She drew in a sharp breath and turned from him. "So long, Fox. I've got to go," she muttered, moving in long, hasty steps up the walk to her door and letting herself inside.

Five

She shut the door and leaned wearily against it. *Research,* she groaned, although the entire purpose behind her decision to pursue a relationship with Brandon was rapidly fading from her mind.

The man was getting to her. No, she debated silently, he'd already gotten to her. There was no point in denying the fact: Brandon Fox had lodged himself in her consciousness in a way that unnerved her. He was right. She desired him.

That wasn't the plan. She was supposed to be trying to gather data for her study. She was supposed to familiarize herself with him, not find herself quaking with longing every time she gazed into his eyes, every time he touched her.

Reliving his touch caused a shudder to grip her. She hoisted up her sweater and yanked the balled-up socks from her bra. Angrily she flung them to the floor. Staring

at the two crumpled white sweatsocks, she forced herself
to acknowledge that they were undoubtedly what Brandon was after. How disappointed he'd be if he ever learned
that Audrey relied on padding for her curvacious figure.

She stooped to pick up the socks, then scanned her living room. How long could she put him off? How long
could she keep him from entering her house? If he'd come
in today, he would have seen the scraps of notes spread
across the coffee table in front of her couch, where she'd
been working on them yesterday afternoon. He'd have
seen the rows and rows of bookshelves lined with
impressive-looking volumes, the professional journals
scattered about her dining-room table. He might have
ventured as far as the spare bedroom, where she stored
even more books and notes.

And if he'd continued to caress her, he'd have discovered the socks. How long would she be able to shove his
hands away from her chest?

How long would she want to? Groaning again, she sank
onto the sofa. His hand against her stomach, against her
waist and her legs, his back pressed up to her, his mouth
on her cheeks, her brow, her lips...Oh Lord, how right he
was in claiming that she wanted him!

She mentally sorted through the afternoon they'd spent
at the campus. The campus...cripes, of all the places he
could have taken her, why had he chosen the campus? All
she could do was be grateful that the fellow who'd spotted her there was a graduate student, used to calling her by
her first name. What if she and Brandon had run into one
of her freshmen students? The freshman would have def-
erentially addressed her as "Dr. Lambert" and her research ploy would have been ended on the spot.

So what about research, she pondered, trying to remain sensible. What had she learned about Brandon Fox that might be of use in her book?

She'd learned that he didn't at all fit the profile of the typical girlie-club customer. *If* he were telling the truth, of course. *If* he were telling the truth about his baking bread and pursuing justice and wanting to be her friend. Could she believe him?

She probably shouldn't. Men were sneaky, and, being a clever man, Brandon was undoubtedly exceptionally sneaky. She ought to know better than to trust him. Her mother trusted her father, and he cheated on her constantly. He was a lawyer too. Lawyers were adept at presenting glib defenses—especially their own.

Her father was dishonest and dishonorable, and so was every other man Audrey had ever known. The classmate she'd dated steadily as an undergraduate had tried to dissuade her from going to graduate school because, he explained, once they were married there would be no point in her being an overeducated housewife. In graduate school she'd thought she was in love with a fellow anthropology student, but then he'd attempted to undermine her research because he was jealous of the acclaim her study received in academic circles. Her favorite professor in college, an utterly brilliant scholar, had tried to blackmail her into sex in return for a high final grade in his course. She'd wound up turning him down and getting a B instead of a well-deserved A—and having her suspicions about men confirmed. Men loved women, sure—as long as women knew their place.

Brandon clearly wanted to convince Audrey that he was different, but why should she let him sway her when she knew better? He'd offered clues of his true feelings a couple of times. He obviously disdained her work at the Angel Club. Apologies notwithstanding, he considered her one step above a harlot. All that rubbish about how she should get her degree and pull herself up by her boot-straps was just rationalization. Apparently he didn't know how to cope with his lust for a woman of a different social caste.

He was an Ivy Leaguer. Proper, well bred, infused with clichés about justice and civil rights. That he desired Audrey didn't fit in with his own self-image, so he had to change Audrey, to make her respectable enough for him.

"Now who's rationalizing?" Audrey chastised herself. She knew what she was doing: searching for reasons to dislike Brandon. Searching for a way to smother the passion he was able to unleash within her.

She *did* want him. She wanted to kiss him forever, to feel his fingers against her skin, to stare into his eyes when they were at their gentlest, a shimmering blend of blue and gray. But she couldn't satisfy such urges while she was busy deceiving him, dissecting him for scholarly ends. If she was going to take the huge risk of trusting him, she'd have to call off the game, find herself another guinea pig, and tell him who she really was.

She wondered how he'd react if she did that. She wanted to believe he'd laugh about it, tell her she was a fine ac-tress, praise her shrewd strategy and her willingness to subject herself to a degrading, unpleasant job at the Angel Club out of devotion to her discipline. But she didn't think that was how he'd take her news. Somehow, she believed he'd be disappointed. He seemed, in his own strangely condescending way, to be enjoying his brush with a woman he considered below his class. She couldn't shake off the understanding that he was as much attracted to the sexy image she presented in her scant Angel Club uniform as in her personality. She hadn't exactly been a sterling companion for him so far.

With a shrug, she resolved to continue to play the game for a little while longer, to see where it would lead them. Her research goals were no longer her top priority when it came to Brandon. But play-acting the role of a waitress seemed to her the safest way to test Brandon's motives. It was her ego she wanted to protect, not her book.

If he telephoned her Monday she wasn't around to receive his call. The university held classes despite the Columbus Day holiday, and in the evening she went to Liz's house for dinner. She left soon after eating, too exhausted to sit up half the night talking to her friend, as she used to do when she wasn't moonlighting as a waitress. She was glad to be able to sleep late Tuesday, since she only taught one seminar which met late in the morning.

Once it was over, she left the campus to do her grocery shopping. She had to shop frequently, because she could tote only one small carton of groceries home on the back of her motorbike. Lugging the carton up the walk, she heard her telephone ringing and quickened her pace.

She dumped the carton onto a kitchen counter and reached for the telephone. "Hello?" she said breathlessly.

"Audrey? It's Brandon," came his familiar voice. "Did I catch you at a bad time?"

"No," she assured him, sinking onto the nearest kitchen chair and swallowing the catch in her voice. It was easier to resist his allure when she wasn't talking to him. "No," she repeated more calmly. "I just got in from the supermarket."

"Well, I hope I'm not too late with this call. I know it isn't much notice, but are you free this evening?"

"This evening?" She ran her fingers nervously over the surface of the small breakfast table beside her and tried to gather her defenses. "What did you have in mind?"

"I've got some wonderful news I want to celebrate with you," he said excitedly. "I just found out I was made a partner in the firm."

"Oh." It took a moment for his announcement to sink in. For a lawyer, being named a partner meant reaching a career pinnacle. It certainly was wonderful news. That Brandon wanted to celebrate with her caught her off guard. "Congratulations!" she declared, hoping her surprise at his invitation wasn't audible.

"Are you available tonight?" he asked again. "I know you don't have to work at the Angel Club."

She stalled, trying to plow through her scrambled thoughts. She simply wasn't sure she should see him, particularly under such festive circumstances. "Aren't you— a little old to be coming up for partner?" she asked.

He didn't reply right away. "A little old?" he finally managed.

"Well—I mean, it's not that you're *old*," she hastened to assure him, "but I thought partner decisions were made after six years. I mean—I figured you were well into your thirties..."

Again he paused before speaking. "I'm thirty-three," he told her. "I took some time off between college and law school and did a stint in the Peace Corps." *The Peace Corps?* Audrey absorbed, but Brandon continued before she could question him. "How do you know about partnership decisions?"

"My father's a lawyer," she said quickly, pleased that it was the truth. "The Peace Corps, huh. You don't seem the type."

"I don't?" He sounded offended. "Why not?"

"Too polished," she told him. "Too...well-groomed. I just can't picture you on your hands and knees in some rice paddy."

He laughed. "In fact, I was on my hands and knees at a construction site in the Dominican Republic. A farmer I'm not." His tone became serious again. "So, about tonight. Can you join me?"

"What's the plan?"

"Dinner. A few toasts to myself."

"Okay—but *just* dinner. Because tomorrow I have—" She stopped herself before blurting out that she had a morning lecture to present at the university. "I have a busy day planned," she completed the sentence.

His silence indicated that he wasn't certain what she was trying to tell him. Probably he inferred that she was warning him not to plan on spending the night. Which was fine with her, she decided. Let him infer that. "Just dinner," he relented. "I'll pick you at six."

"Okay," she said. "I'll see you then."

After bidding him goodbye, Audrey hung up and unloaded the groceries from the carton. But her mind wandered in its own direction. Inviting her to share with him such a special personal occasion implied that Brandon did respect her. Being made a partner in one's law firm was the kind of special event that one shared with one's closest friends, not with some waitress one was trying to bed down for sport. She tried to ward off the trust she felt for him, but it increased within her, vanquishing her doubt. Brandon was apparently earnest about wanting more than just a quick fling with Audrey.

She knew by profession how to analyze human behavior, and his behavior indicated that he wanted something important to develop between them. Bread baker, Peace Corps volunteer, civil rights lawyer...maybe he wasn't a typical man. Maybe she'd finally found the deep, sensitive, moral gentleman she'd long ago given up looking for.

All right. She wasn't foolish enough to deny the obvious. She was attracted to Brandon, and except for their first encounter, he was proving himself to be a decent human being. Perhaps it was time to end the charade, to accept what he was and reveal what she was. If he was as decent as she imagined, then he wouldn't reject her when he discovered that she was an anthropologist starting out on a successful academic career. And if he did reject her, then good riddance to him.

She wasn't quite sure how she'd break the news to him that she wasn't the trampy waitress of his fantasies, but one thing she knew was that she wasn't going to stuff her bra with socks. Let him see her figure as it really was, and if he wasn't too horrified by her rather paltry dimensions, she'd take it from there.

She showered, shampooed her hair and blow-dried it. Then she scoured her closet for an appropriate dress. Her appearance tonight would help to ease her into revealing the truth to him.

She decided on a demure knit sheath of a muted pink. It had long sleeves and a high collar, and it faithfully followed Audrey's lithe curves. A matching pink sash cinched it at the waist. She slipped on a pair of staid leather pumps with modest heels, and fastened an unobtrusive gold chain about her neck. She didn't bother with makeup.

After filling a matching leather purse with a few necessities, she hurried around the living room, hiding as much of the evidence of her career as she could. She couldn't very well remove the numerous books lining the walls. But she gathered up her notes, the student essays that had joined her journals on her dining-room table, and the journals themselves, and carried the items to her spare bedroom. She was shutting the door to the bedroom when Brandon rang for her.

Fortifying herself with a deep breath, she walked to the front door and opened it. Brandon was dressed in tailored brown slacks, a tan corduroy blazer and a crisp cotton shirt unbottoned at the collar. His face radiated his excitement about his career success. He hovered on the threshold for a moment, as if he expected her to bar him from her home. She stepped aside, and he cautiously entered.

He briefly scanned the living-room walls with their multitude of books, and his eyebrows arched in mild surprise. When he turned back to her, his gaze locked onto her chest, and he quirked one eyebrow even higher. "Have you—have you lost weight?" he tactfully asked.

This wasn't going to be easy at all, Audrey acknowledged, feeling her cheeks heat with color. She was suddenly embarrassed for having tricked him, even though the false image she'd presented hadn't been deliberately aimed at him. "I've lost my socks," she mumbled.

His lips twitched in a perplexed smile. "What?"

"My socks," she forced out the words. "I sometimes stuff my bra with socks."

"Why on earth do you do that?"

"Because—because men like big breasts," she explained bluntly. "My fellow waitresses suggested it. It brings better tips."

He seemed momentarily shocked, and then he erupted in laughter. "Oh God, Audrey, what a relief!"

"A relief?" Now it was her turn to be perplexed.

"I thought—" Another deep laugh convulsed him, filling the living room with its deliciously warm music. "I thought there was something wrong with me."

"Wrong with *you*?" This was definitely not the reaction she'd expected.

"I've never in my life been a breast man, Audrey. I always preferred a figure...well, like yours," he concluded, his laughter waning as his gaze coursed down her slender body. His broad grin tempered into a wistful smile of longing. "I much prefer you without your socks," he murmured huskily. "I wish you'd lost them sooner."

He leaned toward her, brushing his lips against her forehead. She automatically tilted her face up, and his mouth captured hers. The fire in his kiss made her forget about the confession she was planning to make, and the apprehension she felt about how he'd react to it. Her confession could wait. All that mattered right now was his kiss.

Pulling her away from the wall, he looped his arms around her and brought her body fully against his. Their tongues dueled playfully but intensely, passion rising rapidly to consume them both. Audrey ran her hands along the cotton of his shirt, feeling the strong contours of his chest beneath the fabric, wondering hazily at the wild craving he aroused within her whenever he kissed her, whenever he held her.

His hands circled her waist, then slid upward to caress her breasts. She didn't pull away; she no longer had to worry about his discovering that her bustline was false. As he moved his palms sensuously over the small swells, her nipples grew taut with arousal. His fingers curved over her flesh, gently kneading it, and her breath escaped her in a desperate gasp.

"We can skip dinner," he murmured before kissing her again.

His hips drove into hers, revealing his eagerness for her, and she gasped again. Her hands tightened reflexively on his shoulders, her fingertips digging into his solid muscles. She battled through her swirling emotions, clinging

free. Silhouette Special Editions — more of what you want from a Romance — more passion, more pleasure, more love.

Escape to where love is the language spoken from the heart. Discover big, powerful, modern stories brought to you by Silhouette's top selling authors. Now as a Regular reader of Silhouette Special Edition you can enjoy 6 superb novels every month from Silhouette Reader Service — delivered direct to your door, post and packing free, with a whole range of special benefits; a free monthly Newsletter, packed with recipes, competitions, exclusive book offers and information on the top Silhouette authors plus extra bargain offers and big cash savings.

And by way of introduction we will send you four specially selected Silhouette Special Edition novels, plus an exclusive Silhouette Tote Bag FREE when you complete and return this card.

Dear Jane,

Your special introductory offer of 4 free books is too good to miss.
I understand they are mine to keep with the FREE Tote Bag.

Please also reserve a Silhouette Special Edition subscription for me. If I decide to subscribe, I shall receive six new books each month for £7.50* post and packing free. If I decide not to subscribe I shall write and tell you within 10 days. The Free Books and Tote Bag will be mine to keep in either case.

I understand that I may cancel my subscription at any time simply by writing to you. I am over 18 years of age.

Name _____

Address _____

_____ Signature _____

Postcode _____ 3S6SE

Jane Nicholls
Silhouette Reader Service
FREEPOST
PO Box 236
Croydon
Surrey
CR9 9EL

NO
STAMP
NEEDED

to the one steadfast notion that before she made love to Brandon she had to tell him the truth about herself. She simply had to; it was only fair.

With a wrenching effort she pulled back from him. "No, Brandon—" she panted. "I think—I think we ought to have dinner first."

His lips curved in a delighted smile. Her statement clearly implied that if dinner came *first*, something else would come later. She hadn't turned him down, she hadn't rejected him, and his pleasure was obvious.

"Whatever you say," he whispered, touching his lips to hers one last time before he released her.

Flustered, she lifted her purse from the coffee table and preceded him out the door, locking it behind them. They strolled hand in hand down the walk to his car and he opened the passenger door for her.

A paper bag lay on the seat, and Audrey lifted it before sitting. It contained two chilled bottles of champagne. "What's this for?" she asked.

He didn't reply until he'd joined her inside the car and turned on the motor. "We're going to Karen's house," he informed her. "She's providing the food, and I'm providing the bubbly. She made partner today too."

Karen? Why did that name ring a bell? Abruptly Audrey remembered: Karen was Brandon's lady friend, the married woman he'd brought with him to the Angel Club. A sharp blade of anger cut through her. "You expect me to have dinner with you and your girfriend?" she exploded.

Brandon chuckled. "She's not my girlfriend," he insisted. "I told you that the night you met her. We work together. We're just close friends." At Audrey's continuing scowl, he added, "Her husband, Tim, will be there too. Honestly, Audrey, there's nothing between me and Karen, nothing but a very close friendship.'' He glanced at her, then backed out of the driveway. ''Don't you believe that men and women can be friends?''

She supposed such a thing was possible, though her own experience with men had always indicated that they couldn't truly treat women as equals—a prime requirement for a solid friendship. But then, this was Brandon, the social-justice, Peace-Corps bread baker. If she was going to trust him, she had to give him the benefit of the doubt when it came to Karen.

Her suspicions were replaced by a sinking disappointment. All afternoon she'd rehearsed the speech she would give Brandon, explaining who she was and what her motives had been with him. In her rehearsals, the scene was to have taken place at a private restaurant table, between her and Brandon alone. She couldn't very well bare her soul in front of Karen and her husband.

She considered asking him to pull the car to the side of the road so they could talk, but he was already turning onto the driveway of a brick split-level only a few short blocks from Audrey's own house. The front door was open, filled with the silhouette of a tall, lanky man who waved as soon as Brandon shut off the engine. There was no opportunity to talk now. Audrey would have to wait until they left Karen's house.

''Tim, this is Audrey,'' Brandon introduced her to the man as they entered the foyer. Tim was a couple of inches taller than Brandon, with dark hair beginning to thin on top and a warm, relaxed smile.

He shook Audrey's hand, then accepted the bag containing the champagne from Brandon. ''Karen?'' he called out as he led them into a spacious living room featuring a wall of brick and modern furnishings. ''The booze has arrived!''

"And not a minute too soon," Karen said as she entered the living room from the kitchen. She wore a casually elegant dress with an apron tied around her waist, and she greeted Audrey with a smile as genuine as her husband's. "Hi, Audrey. I'm so glad we have this opportunity to get to know each other in nicer surroundings. Nothing personal, but the Angel Club wasn't exactly my cup of tea."

"It's designed to cater to men, not women," Audrey pointed out, pondering whether she should drop her little bombshell about her identity in the presence of Karen and Tim. She decided against it. This dinner party belonged to Karen and Brandon, and Audrey didn't want to spoil it with an announcement that might bring on unexpected reactions.

"The Angel Club?" Tim asked in confusion.

"I told you we went there while you were in Boston," Karen reminded him. "Audrey works there." Tim nodded vaguely, and Karen gestured toward the kitchen. "Come on in, everybody, and keep me company. I'm a wreck."

"Why are you a wreck?" Brandon asked as they trooped into the modern kitchen.

"You know damned well why," Karen sniffed as she bent over and opened her oven. She pulled out a casserole dish and studied it intently. "Cooking isn't my forte. Thank God I know how to write up a decent brief. That's my one major talent."

"Oh, you've got other talents," Tim complimented her, giving her rear end a light swat.

She leaped up, brandishing a threatening fist, then laughed and winked at Audrey. "Men," she grumbled confidentially. "Pigs in pants. Where are my cornflakes?" She scanned the counters and located a box. "I hope you don't mind a casserole—I'm pretty sure it's edible. Where I come from, we consider any recipe that comes off the back of a cereal box to be the ultimate in cuisine.'' She sprinkled cornflakes across the top of the casserole dish and shoved it back into the oven.

Tim popped the cork on one of the bottles of champagne and poured the wine into four tulip-shaped crystal goblets, which he distributed. "A toast to the partners," he declared, raising his glass.

"Partners in crime," Brandon exuberantly chimed in, clinking his glass against Karen's and then against Audrey's. "I can't believe the senior partners actually met on a day off just to decide our fate," he mused. "Thornton said they got together yesterday to make decisions."

"Was anyone left out?" Tim asked, leaning comfortably against the counter where Karen was slicing vegetables into a salad bowl.

"Kirk Shambler," Karen answered. "The poor boy spent the day stalking the halls and cursing."

"Is he going to leave the firm?"

"Probably," said Karen with a shrug. She carried the salad bowl through an arched doorway to the dining room, then returned. "Let's not talk shop," she decided. "Bran and I have been yakking law stuff all day. Let's talk about something else." She twisted to face Audrey, giving her a curious inspection. "Boy, you sure look different in real clothes, Audrey. Let's talk about the Angel Club."

"No," Audrey said quickly and firmly. "I don't want to talk shop either."

"Okay," Karen agreed, her smile expanding. "Let's not talk anyone's shop. Let's just get drunk."

As soon as the casserole was done, they assembled around the table to eat. The meal was simple but wholesome, and in fact Tim led the conversation by talking his own shop. He was a mortgage officer at one of the city's banks, and as his discussion about mortgate rate fluctuations and borrowing policies grew more and more complex, Brandon frequently cast Audrey probing looks. She realized that he was concerned about her ability to follow what had become a reasonably esoteric dialogue. She was tempted to stand up and announce that she was a well-read woman with a doctorate degree and that he needn't worry about her intellectual capacity, but she couldn't very well do that. So she bristled beneath his solicitous gaze and kept her mouth shut.

When dinner was done, Karen served coffee and cake and Tim opened the second bottle of champagne. "The night is yet young," Karen commented. "Who's up for some bridge?"

"Oh—I don't think so," Brandon hastily interjected, tossing Audrey another concerned look. "Karen and Tim are bridge fanatics," he explained. "I can just about hold my own. Whenever anyone new walks through their front door, they lasso the sucker in as a fourth. But we don't have to play if—"

A sly smile teased Audrey's lips. In fact she was a superb player. A few rounds of bridge would be a good way to detour Brandon from his patronizing attitude toward her. "That's all right," she assured him and her hosts. "I know the game a little bit. I don't mind playing."

"Are you sure?" Brandon asked as Karen and Tim cleared the table.

"Of course. I haven't played in a while," she told him truthfully. "But I'm certain I remember the rules."

Karen carried two decks of cards and a score pad to the table and sat facing her husband. "We don't have to play for points," Brandon protested.

"It's no fun if you don't play for points," Audrey said testily. She wouldn't tolerate his doting condescension—especially since in this instance it was so misplaced.

He reluctantly took the chair across the table from her. "Do you play any conventions?" he asked cautiously.

"Short club," she replied crisply. "Strong two-club opening."

His eyebrows flickered upward. "Blackwood?"

She smiled complacently, warming to the challenge. "Sliding Roman Blackwood and Sliding Roman Gerber."

He opened his mouth in surprise, then closed it. His mouth twitched into a grin. "I'm not sure I'm familiar with those. I hope I can keep up with you," he muttered, seemingly amused.

The first hand was dealt, and Karen and Tim wound up in possession of most of the high cards. Brandon made a caustic comment about the hosts' failure to treat their guests hospitably as Tim easily bid his game and made it.

After two more deals, Audrey found herself with a splendid hand. Despite Brandon's wary frown, she bid them up to a slam. Once Tim led the first card, Brandon spread his dummy hand onto the table and shrugged. "I hope you know what you're doing," he grumbled as he rose from his chair and circled the table to check her cards.

"You don't have to breathe down my neck," she objected dryly, shooting him an annoyed stare. He obediently backed away, then resumed his seat.

The success of the slam depended on whether or not a finesse would work. Audrey considered the hand carefully, doing a quick mental calculation and deciding that the odds against the finesse were strong. She courageously pulled Brandon's lone ace from the dummy, felling Karen's king. With a triumphant smile, she laid down her hand and claimed the slam.

"Bravo!" Karen cheered her. "Now, admit it, Bran—we do know how to treat our guests."

Brandon was too busy gaping at Audrey to respond immediately. "How did you know to go up with the ace?" he asked in amazement.

"The distribution was weird," she replied, unable to contain a smug grin. "I figure the chances were that the club king would be a singleton. It was a percentage play, but when Tim played the deuce, I got a pretty good picture of Karen's hand."

"Are you sure you didn't peek?" Brandon teased, though he was clearly awed by Audrey's skill. The expected pang of anger at his doubt came and went quickly, and she laughed.

After two rubbers, Audrey apologized about having to leave. "She has a busy day tomorrow," Brandon told his friends as he stood and helped Audrey from her chair. She suspected that his eagerness to leave was based on his hopes about what would happen once he and Audrey were alone.

They thanked their hosts for dinner, and after a few more congratulations from Tim about the partnership decision, Brandon escorted Audrey from the house. He remained silent until they were settled in the car, but instead of turning on the ignition he twisted in his bucket seat to face her. "Why didn't you tell me you were a demon at bridge?" he asked.

She smiled serenely. "It never came up."

"Audrey, you were spectacular. I'm really impressed."

She felt another twinge of anger. "Why should you be so impressed?" she flared, forgetting her resolution to tell him about her education. "You seem to think I'm an ignoramus, Brandon, but I'm not. Just because I'm a waitress doesn't mean I can't play a passable game of bridge."

"Passable?" he snorted at her modest assessment. "Audrey, you creamed them. I'm grateful you brought me along for the ride. Next time we'll have to play them a dollar a point."

"Mercenary, aren't you," she grumbled, her fury abating. Sitting so close to Brandon, inhaling the tangy fragrance of his after-shave, feeling his warmth emanating from his seat to hers, she couldn't stay angry with him. Her own anticipation of what lay in store for them when they arrived at her house pulsed through her, and she hoped that now that Brandon knew she was a fantastic card player he would accept her other news with equanimity. Perhaps he had exhausted his supply of astonishment regarding her, and from here on in, everything she told him would make perfect sense to him.

The drive back to her house was brief, and Audrey said nothing as Brandon accompanied her up the front walk and entered the house behind her. She shut the door, but before she could speak his arms were around her, turning her toward him. His powerful kiss burned through her, blazing away all thought. Her rehearsed speech dissolved instantly in the heat of her yearning.

"Am I rushing you?" he whispered hoarsely, the words touching her cheek like small, bright flames.

Her voice failed her. How could she explain anything when all her mouth seemed capable of doing was kissing him? Later, she vowed, afterward she would tell him. Right now other needs took precedence.

She answered his question by slipping her hand through his and leading him down the short hallway to her bedroom. Before they reached the bed Brandon had her in his arms again, his hands moving languorously down her back and up it again, seeking the zipper of her dress. He slid it open and drew the pink material from her shoulders to her waist.

She pulled her arms from the sleeves, then lifted her eyes to his. He was studying her breasts through the filmy cups of her bra. "You don't even need this," he observed as he reached for the clasp and opened it.

He didn't sound disappointed; she hoped he wasn't. "I need it to hold the socks in place when I'm using them," she pointed out.

He smiled. "In that case, you never need it when you're with me," he murmured, slipping off the bra and tossing it to the floor. His fingers danced up from her waist to her breasts, stroking them reverently. He bowed and kissed one swollen nipple. "You're beautiful," he groaned as his tongue circled the tingling red tip.

She sighed and combed her fingers through his golden hair, holding his head to her as his mouth roamed to the other breast. She felt her energy fleeing from her legs, rising up to her hips and concentrating itself there. Unable to support herself, she dropped onto the edge of the mattress.

He eased the dress over her hips and down her legs, then removed her slip and pantyhose. Straightening up, he stared at her naked body, his gaze moving intimately over her exposed skin. "The most beautiful woman I've ever seen," he breathed. He began to unbutton his shirt, then hesitated. "Do you want to undress me?" he invited her.

She raised her hands to his shirt, but her fingers were trembling too much to function. Brandon smiled and kissed the crown of her head, then hurriedly undressed himself. Within a minute, he was nude.

He joined Audrey on the bed, drawing her alongside himself, and his lips consumed hers in a passionate kiss. His hands traveled the length of her body, pausing at her breasts, at her navel, at the angular protusions of her pelvis, at the silky skin of her inner thigh. Her hands mimicked his, raking through the soft swirls of blond hair that adorned his chest and abdomen, testing the solidity of his muscular legs, reaching for his back and probing its supple lines.

"I've dreamed of this, Audrey," he confessed in a thick, uneven voice. "Ever since the moment I saw you, I've dreamed—"

She cut off his words with another kiss. She didn't want to think of him dreaming about making love to an Angel Club waitress. She ought to stop now, stop everything and tell him that, his dreams notwithstanding, he was making love to an anthropologist, a university professor, an author.

But she couldn't stop. Her body's clamorous urges wouldn't let her. She wanted him too much to halt everything for a serious discussion. *Afterward,* she promised before surrendering completely to their building desire.

His hand settled between her legs, exploring the essence of everything that made her a woman. For right now that was what she was—not a waitress, not a professor, but a passionate woman aching for one man's love. Her hips arched against him and her own hands covered him, discovering what truly made him a man—not a lusting Angel Club customer, not a civil rights lawyer, but a man who ached for her.

His breath grew hard and ragged, and he eased her fully onto her back, pinning her beneath himself. He thrust forcefully into her, and she felt his muscles tensing as he fought for control over the demands of his body. He stopped breathing for a moment, and she saw the strain in his face, felt it in his flesh, knew it in her heart.

He moved inside her, now slow and restrained, and their bodies discovered a natural rhythm. Gradually the tension left his face. Audrey caressed his back with one hand and twined the other into his hair, pulling his face down to hers as their tongues imitated their bodies' movement.

Wave after wave of heady sensation spiraled down and through her, gathering about Brandon, coiling taut. He increased his pace, and Audrey felt as if her soul was being tightened. It burst loose, rippling outward through her flesh to her extremities. She squeezed her eyes shut and cried out. Within an instant, Brandon followed her over the crest.

He remained still for several long minutes, clinging to her, his chest crushing hers as his lungs struggled for air. At last he lifted himself up, propping himself on his arms, and examined her face. "Was..." He swallowed, trying to regulate his breath. "Was it good for you?" he managed.

"Good?" she echoed in disbelief. "Brandon...it was incredible."

He smiled tenuously. "I wanted you so much, Audrey—I couldn't keep from rushing."

Rushing? Compared to her own slim and generally rather dismal past experience, Brandon's lovemaking had been remarkably leisurely and selfless. She tried to think of a way to tell him this. He looked so unnecessarily worried. "It was wonderful," she whispered, cupping her hand to his cheek and smiling.

"I love you," he murmured. She felt him stirring against her thigh. "I want you again. I'll go slower this time, I promise."

Her breath caught in her chest. She couldn't believe he was hungering for her again so soon—or she for him. Simply hearing him confess his desire for her fanned the still-glowing embers of passion inside her into a blaze.

But no—first she had to tell him. Here Brandon was, talking about love, and he still didn't know the truth. "We have to talk," she insisted quietly.

He studied her solemn expression, then accepted her statement and rolled off her, nestling close beside her. "Talk, then," he invited her, nipping her earlobe with his teeth.

She shivered as tongues of fire spread through her body; then she edged slightly from him in order to regain her bearings. "Brandon," she began falteringly. "We—it's important that we both know the truth about each other."

"Of course," he agreed helpfully. "What do you want to know about me?"

Maybe he was offering her the best route to her own honesty: she could ask him something about himself first. "What does the *Q* stand for?"

"The *Q*?" He frowned momentarily, then grinned. "My initial, you mean? Quiller."

"Quiller? What kind of a name is that?"

"It's my mother's maiden name."

"Brandon Quiller Fox," she reflected, deciding that she loved the sound of it. "What's your mother like?"

He chuckled at her line of questioning. "She's a terrific woman. She's a real-estate broker. Very dynamic, successful at just about everything she does."

"How about your father?"

"He's an engineer. Athletic, kind of shy, but generous once he opens up. As parents go, I haven't got any complaints."

How lucky he was, Audrey mused, swallowing her envy. How she wished her mother had been strong enough to forge her own life, respectful but independent of her father. How she wished her father had given her mother that opportunity. How she wished she'd known that two likable parents could produce a son as open and decent as Brandon.

She had to tell him. She had to tell him right now. But suddenly he was kissing her again, his hands floating sensuously over her skin. He stole her breath, her strength, her resolution. She couldn't tell him when he was doing such things to her with his compelling body.

He urged her onto her stomach and hovered above her. "What are you doing?" she whispered.

"Kissing your back," he told her before pressing his mouth to the nape of her neck. His hands massaged her shoulders and sides as his lips worked down the length of her spine. She twisted eagerly beneath him, longing to roll over again, to let him join his body to hers. No man had ever made love to her so thoroughly before; no man had ever taken the time.

When he reached her waist, he lifted his mouth and rearranged his body so he could kiss the dimpled backs of her knees.

She moaned from the insane yearning his kisses kindled. Impatient, she writhed from under him and spun around to face him. He knelt between her knees and teased her navel with his tongue. "Audrey," he groaned, gripping her thighs, pressing his cheek to the flat stretch of her abdomen. "God, I never imagined I could want a woman this much."

"I want you too," she murmured, sliding her hands beneath his arms.

He held back, kissing her stomach again. "Audrey...are you protected?" he asked.

The question stunned her. Her eyes wide with shock, she didn't reply.

He raised himself up to look at her, apparently afraid that he'd embarrassed her. "I'm sorry," he mumbled. "I

really should have asked before, but...I wanted you so
much I couldn't even think. Please don't be angry with me
for asking.''

"I'm...not angry," she managed weakly. She really
wasn't. Just surprised. It wasn't the sort of question men
thought to ask women in the passion of a moment like this.

"I just—I'm the kind of guy who thinks these things are
my responsibility as much as the woman's." He scrutinized her face, trying to decipher her enigmatic expression. He took her silence as an answer, not the one he
would have liked. "I should have asked before," he
muttered.

"No—it's all right," she reassured him. "I mean, it's all
right, Brandon. I'm safe."

He smiled hesitantly. "I guess—I must have assumed
you were," he said, explaining his earlier rashness. "I'm
not a careless person. I guess I knew you would be."

Something uncomfortably cold clawed at her spine, and
she lifted her head off the pillow to confront him. "What
do you mean, you *knew* I would be?"

"I mean...well, given the sort of work you do and all..."

"The sort of work I do?" Her body's temperature
dropped precipitously. She hadn't forgotten about her
promise to tell him the truth about her work, but she
wouldn't tell him now, not when he was insinuating something so—so ugly. "You mean your slimy suspicions about
how I entertain customers after hours?" she spat out.

He had no trouble reading her rage, but he maintained
his poise. "Don't act so indignant, Audrey. I know you're
better than your job at the Angel Club makes you out to
be, but I'm a realist, and I assume you are too. It isn't the
sort of place where they hire documented virgins."

"Brandon—"

"I'm not condemning you," he hastened to defend himself. "I'm only saying that a man tends to make certain assumptions—"

"Get out!" she snapped. "Get out of here! Go away!" She curled into a ball, her back to him, and tried to stifle the many irrational words of fury that rose to her mouth by burying her face in her pillow. High-flown civil rights lawyer indeed! He *was* just a typical Angel Club customer after all. In his gut he believed that women were either madonnas or whores, and any woman who worked at the Angel Club certainly couldn't be a madonna.

He stared at her for a long moment, then reached for her shoulder. At his touch she flinched. "Audrey, don't be this way. I thought we could be honest with each other."

Fat chance of that, she muttered beneath her breath. If she'd been honest with him, he would only have congratulated himself on having picked a proper well-reared professional for his lover. He'd continue to look down his elitist nose at the women who pandered to his true male instincts.

But she wouldn't tell him the truth, certainly not now that he'd revealed the truth about himself. How could she ever have believed he was a better man than the run-of-the-mill male specimens she usually met? He wasn't better. If anything, he was worse. He was a hypocrite.

"Audrey, please—"

"Go away," she ordered him harshly. "I'm going to close my eyes and count to ten. When I open them, you'd better be gone. And yes, I do know how to count to ten, even though I work at a brainless job. Now go." She shut her eyes and began to count. When she reached ten, she opened them and found Brandon seated beside her on the mattress. "Do you understand English?"

"I *don't* understand you," he countered softly.

"That's your hard luck, buster. It's actually quite easy to understand. I work at the Angel Club, so you assume I'm a slut. Now you've lived out your little-boy fantasy, so you're free to go. Go back to your proper ladies. Or maybe you'd rather find yourself another slut with *real* breasts—"

"Stop it," he growled.

"I won't stop till you get out of here," she warned, her voice going up an octave but quavering at the end.

"I'm on my way," he complied in an emotionless tone, warily containing his own anger. He rose from the bed and gathered his clothes. Audrey pulled her blanket over her and glowered at him while he dressed.

"And don't send me any more flowers!" she hurled at him as he approached the door. "Go find yourself another tramp to drool over!" He left the bedroom, slamming the door behind himself.

Audrey dropped back onto the pillow and succumbed to a slow sob. Men, she thought. What had Karen called them? Pigs in pants, that was it. They were all the same.

Audrey was relieved that she hadn't confessed her deception to Brandon. If anything could be salvaged from this evening, if she ever recovered her wits, she'd have some invaluable insights to use in her work. *If* she recovered. But the way she felt, distraught and miserable and seething with hurt, that wasn't at all a certainty.

Six

___

He got as far as her living room and stopped. If he walked out of Audrey's house, he'd be walking out of her life, and he wasn't willing to do that. She'd overreacted to his dumb remark. He was sure they could work it out once she calmed down.

He tossed his blazer onto her sofa and surveyed the room. The furniture, while not new, looked homey and comfortable. The built-in bookcases covering the walls had taken him by surprise when he first entered the house, and he turned to one to inspect her library. Franz Boas, Ruth Benedict, Margaret Mead, Desmond Morris, Carlos Casteneda—not exactly escapist reading. Mingled in with the anthropological classics was equally serious literature—Shakespeare, Dickens, Proust, Austin, Henry Adams and Henry James. Audrey was obviously well read. Unless, of course, she was one of those people who viewed books as part of her home's decor and filled her shelves with scholarly treatises simply because they looked right.

That was a snobbish thought, Brandon reproached himself. Just one more snobbish thought on his part. Whenever he hurt Audrey's feelings—and he seemed to have a special talent when it came to that, he reflected morosely—it was because he said something that she viewed as degrading or condescending. She believed he was patronizing her, even though that was never his intention.

All he'd done was imply that when it came to sex he naturally assumed she'd be prepared. He hadn't meant that as an insult; modern women were frequently prepared for sex. But to Audrey his remark had been an insult because she still hadn't forgiven him for the equally insulting implication he'd voiced the first night they met. She was sensitive about her work at the Angel Club, so sensitive that she couldn't take Brandon's comment about contraception as anything but a slur against her.

He'd never doubted that women were a complicated breed, but he'd always assumed that the most complex women were those he generally associated with: white collar professionals like himself. That too was a snobbish thought, he acknowledged. But he'd rarely had any dealings with women who *weren't* white collar professionals. He admitted ruefully that he tended to judge other sorts of women who were less well educated, less ambitious— waitresses and barmaids and so on—as somehow simpler.

But Audrey was the most confusing woman he'd ever met. Her books indicated intellectual tastes, and her ability at bridge revealed an astute analytical brain. And yes, she was perceptive enough to understand Brandon even better than he understood himself. She was painfully aware of his snobbery, even when he meant no offense with his words.

As she was aware of his snobbery she was also aware of his ignorance about women like her, and his veiled—and sometimes not so veiled—patronizing attitude toward her. That was what she'd been reacting to in the bedroom. That was why her anger had erupted all out of proportion to what he'd said.

He'd also said he loved her, and even now, when they seemed farther apart than ever before, he believed that he'd spoken the truth. It wasn't rational, but love didn't have to be rational. He loved Audrey. He loved her body and her mind. He loved her supersensitivity. He loved her nerve. To work at a place like the Angel Club took a courage and stamina that he admired. To ride the streets of Albany on a motorcycle took fearlessness. To rise with the dummy's ace during a tricky slam bid at bridge took a bravery Brandon himself didn't possess.

He'd lived an easy life. He came from a loving, close-knit family, had all the advantages of a comfortable childhood and a superior education. He'd learned about injustice by reading about it, not by living it. His two years in the Peace Corps had taught him plenty about injustice, about the cruelty of poverty and the danger of ignorance in a country's populace, but the only dirt that had actually touched him had been the soil he'd dug up and the concrete he'd laid down for the rural schoolhouse he'd helped to build. Even as a Peace Corps volunteer he'd been detached from life's harshness. He knew that once his time was served he'd be able to rejoin the cushy world he'd always known, filled with pride about his good deeds.

Audrey was correct in viewing him as a snob, although she was wrong about his fantasies. When it came to her, his fantasies were much the same as his dreams when he'd been in the Dominican Republic—he wanted to save those people from their own miserable existence, and he wanted to save Audrey.

If that wasn't patronizing, nothing was, he confessed to himself ruefully.

He heard a door opening down the hall, and turned to see Audrey gliding toward him. She wore a velour wrap-around robe of a muted raspberry shade, and as he'd contemplated earlier that evening, the color pink suited her, emphasizing her dark hair and eyes, and her clear pale skin.

She didn't seem surprised to find him loitering in her living room. Without speaking, she moved directly into the kitchen. Brandon followed her.

He watched her prowl silently about the room, filling a kettle with water and setting it to boil on her range, then spooning loose tea into a porcelain teapot. Waiting for the water to heat, she raked her fingers haphazardly through her tangled waves of hair, brushing them back from her face. Brandon imagined his own hands in her hair, and he had to fight back the rush of longing that the thought evoked. The kettle issued a shrill whistle, shattering his reverie.

Audrey emptied the water into the teapot and swirled it around. She glanced at Brandon and pulled two mugs from a cabinet. After pouring the tea, she carried the mugs to the round breakfast table by the window. "Do you take anything in it?" she asked softly.

He shook his head and dropped onto one of the chairs. She seated herself across from him and gazed at the steam rising from her cup.

"Why do I constantly feel as if I've got to apologize to you?" he asked.

"Probably because you do," she muttered before raising her mug to her lips.

"You know, there's nothing wrong with a woman's taking precautions," he commented gently, moderating his voice to disguise his frustration. "I meant it as a compliment. A smart woman doesn't leave things to chance."

Audrey glared dubiously at him, then sipped again from her mug. "It just so happens, Fox, that I've been on birth control pills since I was sixteen. I have a hormone imbalance, and the pills counteract it. But I'm sure you don't believe that. You probably believe I was already a sexual libertine at that age."

Again he was struck by her speech, her choice of words. His curiosity about her seemed boundless. She'd been to college and was continuing her education now. Her father was a lawyer. Possibly her background wasn't much different from Brandon's. Yet she'd wound up living such a different life. "Why do you keep talking about madonnas?" he asked, recalling not only what she'd said in bed but what she'd said during their picnic at the campus several days ago—something about how her father had taught her her ridiculous notions about how men viewed women.

"Because you're a man," she retorted. "Men divide women into the chaste types and the easy types: madonnas and whores."

"I don't do that," he insisted, a flicker of anger burning in his eyes. "You don't like when I make incorrect presumptions about you, Audrey. Well, I don't like it when you do that to me. You seem to have some pretty strong prejudices when it comes to men, and I don't like it. You're worse than you claim men to be; you don't even bother to divide us into two camps. You lump us all together. I don't think that's fair."

"Fair?" she scoffed, then scowled sheepishly. "All right," she conceded. "It isn't fair. Life isn't fair. I'm speaking from experience, Fox."

"What experience? The nonsense your father fed you?"

"That and more. You're just the latest example in a string of them, I'm afraid. I see the proof every night; I see the way men's minds function, the way they view me. I work at the Angel Club; therefore I must be a tramp, popping birth control pills and looking for fun."

"*I* never said that."

"In your own charming way, you did," she argued. A deep sigh slipped past her lips. "I don't want to fight with you, Brandon. I'm just trying to be realistic here. We're not good for each other."

"We were good for each other in the bedroom," he murmured. "Before everything fell apart."

Her large eyes glued themselves to his. "Oh, you mean you're an expert lover so I should forgive everything else?"

"I think..." He paused to sort his thoughts. "I think that what happened between us in bed ought to wipe the slate clean, Audrey. I love you."

She snorted. "You're handy with words, Fox," she allowed. "Maybe you think you have to say you love me so I'll give myself to you. That's another typical thing with men. They think that if they make the right speech to women, if they swear their undying love, they'll automatically receive absolution for their sins. I grew up watching that sort of garbage, Brandon, but it doesn't work for me. My father's a lawyer, I told you that. He's handy with words too. Every day he tells my mother he loves her. In his own myopic way he probably believes that he does. He sends her flowers, and he tells her he loves her."

"And?"

"And then he runs around with flashy bleached blondes. He flies off to Bermuda for a weekend with some woman with big breasts. He wines and dines his clients at joints as trashy as the Angel Club. Then he brings my mother a big bouquet and says, 'I *do* love you, Martha. I honestly do.'"

Brandon pressed his lips together. Audrey's bitterness and cynicism about men were deeply ingrained. He didn't know how to go about convincing her she was wrong, how to counteract the gritty education life had handed her. "What does your mother do?" he asked.

"Nothing," Audrey said dully. "When he traipses off to Bermuda, she believes him when he tells her it's business. When he doesn't roll home until two A.M., she believes him when he swears that he was out having a few drinks with one of his colleagues. She sits at home, in the nice big house he bought for her, and arranges the flowers he brings her. She figures she ought to count her blessings that such a wonderful guy loves her so much."

"So you think you can solve everything by being the exact opposite of her?" Brandon asked shrewdly. "You think that by closing your heart to every man you'll wind up happier than her?"

"I think," Audrey replied testily, "that I'm better off not making her mistakes. She has nothing but flowers. At least I've got a career."

"At the Angel Club? You consider that a career?"

Audrey's lips flexed, and her eyes darted toward the window. "I mean," she said, fidgeting with her cup, "that I've got my own life. And I'm content with it. I'm not so dependent on some man that I have to put up with that kind of emotional neglect and abuse."

"You've worked it out very neatly," Brandon muttered sarcastically. "But the truth of the matter is, you were worlds happier a half hour ago in my arms than you are now." Before she could dispute him, he continued. "You've got such a wall of resistance built around you, Audrey, that you aren't even willing to peek past it and see that I'm not like your father. I'm certainly not perfect—I've made more than my share of mistakes with you. But...but I care for you. I deserve another chance.''

"How many chances do you deserve, Fox?" she snapped. "I've already given you several."

Once again he felt a strange compulsion to save her. Not from her job this time, but from the bitterness that blinded her to the joy he knew they could find together. "One more chance," he implored her.

She stared thoughtfully at him. He sensed a hairline crack in her resistance, and he prayed for it to spread wide enough for her spirit to seep through. "I...don't know," was all she would concede.

It was better than a total rejection, he tried to console himself. He drained his mug and lowered it to the table with a thud. "Okay," he announced. "I'm a lawyer. Here's my case: I think you're special. I think you're a terrific woman. I think you've experienced some pain in your past, but I think you're strong enough to overcome it. I want to help you to overcome it—and no, I'm not being a snob when I say that. I'm just being a man, a man who cares about you."

"You like making little speeches, don't you," she observed dryly.

"I'm just laying my hand on the table."

"Like a dummy at bridge," she sniffed. "Okay, you've laid down your hand. I sure as hell wish you could remember all your noble intentions when you're about to put your foot in your mouth. Because your real feelings keep sneaking through at the wrong times."

She could be right about that, he admitted silently. She could be right in asserting that his real feelings were that she *was* a prostitute, a loose woman, someone who needed him to make her respectable. Yet he wanted to believe he was the man of his "little speeches." He wanted to believe he'd be good for her. As odd as it seemed, he already knew that Audrey was good for him. She forced him to confront his own biases and shortcomings. She called him a snob when that was exactly what he was. "I need you," he confessed. "I need you to remind me where to put my foot and where not to put it."

She laughed grimly. "You don't need me tonight, Fox. You've already had me. Maybe it's time for you to leave."

Obviously this discussion had been difficult for her. Brandon knew he couldn't probe further, couldn't resolve anything with her right now. So he would prove his respect for her by abiding by her wishes. "All right," he yielded. "I'll leave. But this isn't goodbye, Audrey. I hope you recognize that."

She rolled her eyes. "Stop making speeches," she told him. "See how you feel in the morning. You may be inclined just to put another notch in your belt and call it history."

"No," he argued, but her steady stare disconcerted him and he decided it best not to say anything more. Later, after they'd both reflected on what had happened, they could approach each other sensibly. Once Audrey wasn't so furious with him, he'd be able to prove that his feelings for her were genuine.

He carried his mug to the sink and then strode to the living room for his blazer. When he returned to the kitchen he found Audrey where he'd left her, sitting at the cozy table, her tapered fingers curled about her mug, her eyes riveted to him. "Good night," he murmured.

"Good night, Brandon."

It took enormous willpower not to cross the room to her, to kiss her, to touch her. He hated leaving her when she looked so desolate, but she wasn't giving him any choice. So he purposefully turned and left the house.

"Bran? Can I come in?"

Brandon peered up from the thick wad of papers which had arrived for him in the morning mail. Karen was inching his office's door open. He waved her inside, and she swung the door shut behind herself and walked over to the plush leather chair facing him at his broad mahogany desk.

"The standard routine," she teased, "is that you're supposed to thank your hostess for the lovely dinner last night."

"Thank you," Brandon obeyed. "I'm not sure cream-of-mushroom soup à la cornflakes qualifies as lovely, but thank you."

Karen laughed at his succinct criticism of the meal she'd prepared. "Tim and I had a marvelous time, Bran. We were very impressed with Audrey."

Brandon gritted his teeth to contain the discomfort the mention of Audrey's name provoked. "I'm glad you liked her."

"Except for her having trounced us at bridge," Karen cheerfully complained. "You should have warned us she was a whiz before we took her on." At his silence, she leaned forward. "Bran, was I seeing things, or did her figure change? I mean, is it something about that uniform she had to wear at work that made her look so...so—"

"Surely you didn't come in here to discuss Audrey's mammary glands with me," Brandon muttered impatiently.

Karen noticed his uneasiness and scowled. "What's eating you?"

"She is," he confessed, letting his chin sink wearily against his cupped palms.

"She didn't enjoy the dinner?"

"The dinner was fine."

"Something happened afterward?"

"Afterward was fine...up to a point. Then everything fell apart." He sighed. "I don't know whose fault it was. She seems to think we're bad for each other. I think...I think we could be very good for each other. I suppose that's a pretty big issue for us to disagree about."

Karen assessed him critically. "You're really hooked on her, aren't you."

He nodded grimly. "Do you think I'm crazy?" he asked.

"Before last night I might have. But Audrey isn't at all what I expected her to be. My first impression of her was that she was...well, what she appeared to be: a floozy waitress. She isn't, though. I don't know what her story is, Bran, but if you're hooked on her, you're hooked on her." She waited for him to comment. When he remained silent, she asked, "Why does she think you're bad for each other?"

"She thinks I'm a snob. She thinks I look down my nose at her."

"You? Brandon 'Mr. Liberal' Fox?"

"She's right," he noted glumly. "It's not that I *mean* to be a snob, but then things slip out. She seems to believe that what's slipping out are my true feelings. Maybe she's right. I always thought I was 'Mr. Liberal' too, Karen, but it was easy to be a liberated man when I was dealing with like-minded women. Audrey's different. I just don't know what to think about her, how to act around her."

Karen's eyebrows dipped in a frown. "This doesn't sound like you at all, Bran. I've never seen you so torn up over a woman before."

"I've never before felt for a woman what I feel for Audrey. I'm in love with her, Karen, but maybe she's right in thinking my feelings are an outgrowth of some latent superiority complex."

"She said that?"

"Not in so many words," he mumbled. No way was he going to tell Karen what Audrey really had said, about his little-boy fantasies and all that.

Karen appraised the situation. "Maybe you ought to send her some more flowers," she advised.

"God, no. That was the worst idea in the world," he retorted. "Her father sends her mother flowers. There's all sorts of ghastly significance involved in it."

"Uh-oh," Karen groaned. "I'm not going to say another word on the subject. It's much too complicated for me, thank you. You've got my best wishes for good luck and a long and happy future with her, and I'll leave it at that." She eyed the papers on his desk with curiosity. "What's all this stuff?"

The papers spread before him gave him a chance to take his mind off Audrey. "An associate professor in the English department at SUNY-Albany organized a petition drive in support of our position in the Capital Club case." He skimmed the cover letter, locating a name. "Elizabeth Simpson. She also pressured two university deans into resigning from the club—she's forwarded photocopies of their letters of resignation—and she's willing to offer further support and assistance in the case."

"Wow!" Karen gathered up the petition and scanned it. "Not bad, not bad at all. Have you talked to her?"

"I left a message for her in the English department office this morning. She was teaching a class."

"Two deans quit, huh?" Karen grinned appreciatively. "Are you going to share this with Prager?"

"Of course. I know our clients want to go to trial, but I'd just as soon avoid it if we can succeed without it. As soon as you remove your butt from my office I intend to call Prager and tighten the screws."

"I'm on my way," Karen complied, rising and heading for the door. "Give him hell, Bran."

"Will do," Brandon called after her as she pulled the door shut.

He flipped his Rolodex to Prager's number and dialed. As soon as he identified himself to the secretary at the other end, she put the call through. "Fox!" Prager bellowed amiably. "To what do I owe the honor of this call?"

"To the fact that at this very minute, as we speak, I'm holding a petition signed by four hundred twenty-three staff and faculty members at SUNY-Albany protesting the exclusion of women from the Capital Club."

Prager harrumphed. "Academic liberals," he muttered.

"There's more, Prager—two deans resigned from the club."

"Mmm, I heard a rumor about that." Prager coughed uneasily. "Okay, two deans. Let's talk turkey, pal. The Capital Club's membership roll is loaded with state legislators, bureaucrats, bankers, executives, big wheels and V.I.P.s. A couple of university deans may lend some highbrow prestige to the club, but they haven't exactly got the financial clout most of the members have. Their defection may be a minor embarrassment, but it doesn't change things much."

"In other words, your people aren't going to budge?"

"I don't know. What else have you got up your sleeve?"

Brandon glanced at the letter he'd received from Professor Simpson. "I'm not going to lay out my arsenal for your inspection, Prager," he said ominously. "But we could be discussing *major* embarrassments."

"What? Are a bunch of flaky feminists going to burn their bras on the front step of the club's headquarters? That could spice things up."

Brandon stifled the urge to verbalize his disgust. "Look, Prager, I don't want things to get nasty and neither do you. Your people have an indefensible position—"

"Like hell they do," Prager returned haughtily. "What we're dealing with is the very nature of private clubs in America."

"We're dealing with a business club, Prager, and you know it. I should think the membership would be mortified to lose two upstanding members like Dean Willis and Dean Goldberg."

"I tell you what," Prager said in an placating voice. "Let me talk to my side and get back to you. I'm scheduled for a powwow with the board tomorrow morning. How about you and I meet for dinner? Maybe I'll have something to report."

"Dinner tomorrow." Brandon flipped open his leather-bound appointment calendar. "Fine," he agreed, penciling in the engagement.

"We can meet at six," Prager suggested. "How does the Angel Club suit you?"

"Terribly," Brandon quickly declined. "I don't like that place."

"Oh come off it, Fox, you loved it. All those tasty little waitresses—"

A hot wave of rage surged through him. "No, Prager. Not the Angel Club."

"You seemed to enjoy it plenty the last time we went there."

"I did not!"

Prager laughed. "Your eyes were popping out of their sockets, Fox. Don't play games with me. I'm on to you. I know you fancy yourself the proper gentleman, but our cute waitress had you dancing in your pants. Admit it, pal.''

What had Karen said? Something about wanting to string Prager up by his thumbs? Brandon could easily understand her feelings. Yet he couldn't deny that Prager's success in riling him lay in the fact that his arrow had struck very near the mark. While he wouldn't agree with Prager's coarse phrasing, Audrey had certainly had an incredible effect on him. "The truth is, Prager, I don't want to go there.''

"Not enough of a man to take it?'' Prager goaded him. "Representing those domineering broads has turned you into a sissy, is that it?''

Something snapped inside Brandon. It didn't matter how liberated a man was—when another man threatened his manhood, reflexive juices flowed. "The Angel Club it is, then,'' he growled, adding a silent curse.

"Wonderful. I'll meet you there at six,'' Prager said before hanging up.

Brandon stared at the dead receiver in his hand. He would have to call Audrey to explain, he realized. He'd have to phone her and explain that he would be at the restaurant tomorrow, and that it had nothing to do with little-boy fantasies, but rather with legal strategies, with being able to take on his adversary anytime, anywhere, any way. He'd have to explain that what was going on between the two of them shouldn't be influenced by his appearing at the club while she was on duty.

He hung up the phone, then reached for his wallet to pull out Audrey's number. But his phone began to ring, and when he answered it his secretary announced that Dr. Simpson from the university was on the line, returning his call. Brandon settled in his chair and asked the secretary to connect the call.

"Mr. Fox?" a bubbly soprano lilted through the wire. "Hi, this is Liz Simpson at Albany State. I got a message that you called me this morning."

"Yes, Dr. Simpson. I received the petition you sent me, and the photocopies of the deans' letters of resignation. I must thank you for organizing this drive on behalf of our clients."

"Well, I know one of them—Gilda Ramsey. She's a neighbor of mine, and a good friend. She's told me about her membership application being rejected from the club a few times, and I'm indignant on her behalf."

"So are a number of your colleagues at the university, judging by the petition," Brandon noted.

"Anything that will help," the professor offered. "I hate discrimination in all its forms. What else can we do for you?"

"That's a good question," Brandon mused. "What did you have in mind?"

"Letters to the editor. Letters to the Capital Club. Demonstrations. Rallies. You name it."

He was stunned by her enthusiasm. "Dr. Simpson—"

"Call me Liz," she insisted. "Everybody does."

"All right, Liz," he agreed. "But when it comes to making statements, I plan to refer to you as Dr. Simpson. It sounds more authoritative."

"Ha!" She chuckled. "Don't let anyone know that I teach mostly freshman composition courses. So what can we do for you?"

"Maybe we ought to give the various possibilities some thought and then get together to chew them over. I'd like to bounce a few ideas off my boss—my senior partner," he corrected himself. He still wasn't accustomed to thinking of himself as Thornton's equal in the firm. "When can we set up a meeting?"

"Tomorrow's no good for me," Liz reported. "But Friday's pretty empty. How about after lunch? Say, one o'clock?"

"I could take you out to lunch," he invited her.

"Thanks, but no. I've got to lose a few pounds. One o'clock. My office is in the Humanities building, third floor. That's the building on the southwest corner of the Podium."

"One o'clock," Brandon confirmed, penciling the appointment into his calendar. "I'm looking forward to it. And thanks again. You must be a wonderful friend of Ms. Ramsey to do all this for her."

"I'm doing it for all women everywhere," Liz announced grandly. "As I said, I don't like discrimination."

"Neither do I. I'll see you Friday," Brandon signed off. Dropping the receiver into its cradle, he chuckled. He'd bet his last dollar that this Liz Simpson and Karen would adore each other if they ever met. Fiery feminists, the two of them, itching for fights.

Women like that he could understand. Women like Audrey...God, he'd give anything to be able to understand her. His humor dissipated as he contemplated the beautiful, mysterious woman who had entered his life and turned it upside down. Why couldn't she be another fiery feminist?

Perhaps she was. Perhaps she was the genuine article, a real woman who had to face the indignities women like Karen and Professor Simpson only theorized about. It was easy enough to organize petition drives when one didn't have to confront the insult of sexism every day. A lawyer, a college professor—what did they know about the life Audrey lived, slaving every night at the Angel Club?

If only he could convince her that his respect for her was far greater than it was for women like Professor Simpson. If only he could prove that he respected Audrey not only for her strength and determination, but for her willingness to expose his own weaknesses and thus forcing him to deal with them. If only he could prove to her that they were good for each other, that they needed each other, that he loved her not only in spite of what she was but because of it...

Sighing, he pulled out her number and dialed it. No one answered. He hung up, sighed again and left his office to talk to Thornton about the college professor's strategies for combatting the Capital Club.

Seven

Audrey dropped the sheaf of typed pages onto the coffee table and groaned. She had spent nearly an hour on the phone with her editor that morning, listening to him nag her about sending him some new material and revisions for her book. She'd promised to have something in the mail for him by the following Monday.

The information she'd written up based on her acquaintanceship with Iris and the other waitresses was excellent; just a few more after-work get-togethers with one or two of the other women would round out the picture beautifully.

But the pages she'd composed concerning Brandon.... She stared dismally at the stack of paper on the table before her and groaned again. No. She couldn't use it. It wasn't accurate. It wasn't fair.

He claimed that she wasn't being fair with him, and he was right. He'd been right about many things last night.

Especially when he accused her of being guilty of the same fault she found in men: an unwillingness to judge members of the opposite sex as individuals, and instead a tendency to lump them into camps. She didn't doubt the accuracy of her past research; she knew her profile on girlie-joint customers was properly drawn. But simply because such a type existed didn't give her the right to force Brandon to fit the profile. His visits to the Angel Club couldn't automatically make him something he wasn't.

He'd been right in saying that she was prejudiced against men. He'd also been right in asserting that she'd been happy in his arms. If he'd been the sort of person her statistics insisted that he was, she would never have made love with him.

But she had. She'd made love with him, freely, ecstatically, joyfully. She'd let him see her body as it really was and he'd loved her for it. He had said he loved her, and she believed him. She loved him too.

He was wrong in arguing that she lumped all men into one category. In truth she divided the male species into two groups: the creeps, and her imaginary ideal of men who accepted that women were their equals and treated them with respect. The sorry fact was that such perfection didn't exist, and if she kept comparing every man she met to her ideal conception of manhood, living, breathing men would always fall short. In her own way she'd categorized men into the male equivalent of madonnas and whores.

Brandon was neither. He admitted that he wasn't perfect, but she had no right to demand perfection of him. And last night her heart had told her something her mind would simply have to accommodate: she loved Brandon even though he wasn't perfect.

He'd made his mistakes, but he was honorable enough to acknowledge them and apologize for them. He was strong enough to want to change his attitudes for her.

There was a limit to how far she could fight the truth. It would be easier for her to ignore her emotions, and to continue to cling to her preconceptions about men. But it would also be dishonest. Her heart possessed a wisdom that years of observing men and battling them had concealed from her. Yet even before last night she'd seen the glimmerings of that wisdom. She'd resisted giving in to her feelings, but she couldn't do that anymore. It wasn't right. Brandon had protested that she wasn't being fair, and as she reflected on it, she understood how correct he'd been. If she denied her love for him, she'd be unfair not only to him but to herself.

She had to explain to him. She had to apologize, just as he'd apologized to her. Rising from the sofa, she strode to the kitchen to telephone him, to confess her love, to beg his forgiveness.

As she reached for the telephone she glimpsed the wall clock and cringed. It was already after one A.M. She couldn't call him now and wake him up. Tomorrow, she decided. Tomorrow, when they were both wide awake and refreshed, she'd call him and tell him the truth—the whole truth about herself, about her research, and her love.

Unfortunately she had no way to reach him during the day; she didn't know where he worked. She resolved to phone him at his home during one of her breaks at the Angel Club that evening. All day, while teaching her graduate seminar, while contacting Liz and getting her to agree to proofread the chapter on the waitresses, while meeting with students during her office hours, a part of her mind concentrated on Brandon, on the call she would make that evening, and the many truths she would reveal to him. She would tell him she loved him and trusted him. She would tell him she knew he wasn't a typical Angel Club fan, a leering little boy with fantasies. She would tell him she respected him as much as he claimed to respect her. It would be her turn to make a little speech; she hoped he'd be more receptive to it than she'd been to his.

Confessing her love to Brandon excited and frightened her. She was riddled with anxiety when she arrived at the club, but her certainty that she was doing the right thing helped to quell her edginess. She felt none of her usual revulsion as she slipped on her skimpy uniform and jammed her socks into the low-cut front of the leotard. She was too distracted by thoughts of Brandon to feel any of the distaste she usually suffered when she arrived at the club.

She wandered among the tables of early arrivals, behaving as calmly as she could while her mind bubbled with thoughts of Brandon. She checked her wristwatch frequently. Maybe at around seven she'd be able to take a break and phone him.

Then suddenly she saw him. For an instant she thought she was hallucinating, her brain so keyed into him that she might merely have mistaken the tall, blond customer standing by the hostess's podium for him. But no, she couldn't be mistaken. The man in the neatly tailored gray suit and striped maroon tie was definitely Brandon. His sharp glance when he spotted her across the dining room froze her in place.

She recognized the stocky man with him. He'd been with Brandon that first night at the club; Brandon had said something about their being on opposite sides of a lawsuit. The plump man was conferring quietly with the hostess, and Audrey watched with increasing horror as the hostess nodded and smiled and escorted them to a table in Audrey's station.

Obviously Brandon hadn't come here to see her. He was here as a customer, an Angel Club patron. Maybe he *had* come here to see her, she fumed. Maybe he'd come to see her hideous uniform, with her upholstered chest and her sexy mesh stockings.

That the two men were business associates didn't mean much to her. That they might be having another business dinner was irrelevant. There were countless other restaurants in Albany at which they could meet to discuss business over dinner. But no, they'd come here, to the Angel Club. Audrey intuitively knew that what the plump man had been asking the hostess was to be seated at a table Audrey served. The men hadn't come here to eat; like most of the other customers, they'd come here to gawk. At her. At Audrey.

Brandon continued to stare at her as he took his seat. He finally turned from her when his companion said something to him, and Audrey raced to the kitchen to recover her wits. *Hypocrite!* she raged silently, gripping the stainless steel salad counter to still her trembling hands. Hypocrite! She could think of no good reason on earth that Brandon would have come here. But she had little difficulty thinking of many bad reasons. In the few weeks she'd been working at the club, he'd already visited three times. If that didn't mark him as a frequent customer, a typical girlie-joint creep, nothing did.

Oh sure, he was full of high-minded emotion when he wanted to seduce Audrey. Like any successful lawyer, he'd use whatever worked to persuade his opponent to accept his position. In Audrey's case, taunting her about being a prostitute hadn't worked, so he'd altered his strategy and presented himself as an open, dignified gentleman. And he'd succeeded. He'd scored with the saucy waitress in the seductive silver uniform. He'd probably done just as she'd advised him to do the other night—notched his belt and patted himself on the back.

She couldn't hide from him all evening, though. She had a job to do. Gritting her teeth, she strode out of the kitchen and approached the table where Brandon and the plump man were seated. She'd do her job, yes, but she wouldn't exert herself by being pleasant about it.

"Would you care for drinks before you order?" she asked coolly, focusing solely on the plump man.

He offered her a broad grin. "Hello, Audrey, remember us?" he cooed. "How's my favorite new angel?"

"Fine," she muttered, her scowl belying her words.

He chuckled and shook his head. "Now, now, Audrey—you were supposed to say we were your favorite customers. But I'll forgive you because you look so scrumptious tonight. Doesn't she look scrumptious, Fox?"

Audrey risked a quick glance at Brandon. He glowered at the other man. "Lay off, Prager," he snapped before turning back to Audrey. His expression became pleading, his gentle gray-blue eyes struggling to communicate some unvoiced message. But though he flexed his lips several times, he said nothing.

"Would you care for a drink, *sir*?" she recited tensely, emphasizing the word to distance herself from him.

Again he flexed his lips, then whispered, "A Beck's, thank you."

"One Beck's," she repeated, spinning back to the plump man. "And you?"

"A stinger."

Without another word she marched from the table to the bar. Waiting impatiently for the bartender to fill the order, she nervously shifted her weight from foot to foot. As during Brandon's other visits to the restaurant, she was acutely aware of his eyes on her, watching her, ogling her.

How in the world could she have believed that he loved her? He only loved her the way her father loved his mistresses. She was an object of Brandon's fantasies, no more, no less. His presence at the club proved it. He had come back to fantasize some more.

When she carried their drinks to the table, she found the men engaged in a serious conversation. But they quickly fell silent at her arrival, and the plump man presented her with another drooling smile. "My friend Fox here can't keep his eyes off you," he announced cheerfully.

Audrey sensed Brandon cringing, but she resolutely refused to look at him. "It sounds like quite a problem," she quipped dryly. "Perhaps he should visit an ophthalmologist."

The plump man guffawed and slung his arm around Audrey's waist. "Do you believe it, Fox? Beauty and wit rolled into one. Where have you been all my life, sweetheart?"

"Take your hand off her," Brandon snapped.

The plump man appeared amused by Brandon's gruff command, but before he could respond, Audrey turned on Brandon. "What's your problem, buster?" she railed. "Don't you think I know how to remove his hand if I want to? I don't need you to protect me."

Brandon sank back in his seat, his frown deepening. The plump man laughed again. "Beauty, wit and spirit. Audrey, sweetie, I think I'm in love. You wouldn't by any chance be free after hours, would you?"

"No," she said, her eyes fixed on Brandon. "No, I'm afraid my evenings are booked for the rest of my life."

"I can't say that news surprises me," the plump man said. "But do let me know if someone cancels out and you can squeeze me in." He let his arm drop from her, though his smirk remained plastered across his face. "I would consider it the honor of a lifetime if you would bat those big brown eyes of yours in my direction someday."

She managed a smile that was really more of a sneer before telling the men she'd be returning in several minutes to take their dinner orders. Then she hastened from the table.

A platter of dinners for one of her other tables was awaiting her in the kitchen, but she didn't think she had the strength to lift the tray. She stared blindly at it, struggling to regain her composure.

"Hey, Audrey, what's up?" Iris asked as she reached for her own tray. "You look like you've just seen a ghost."

"You're not far from the mark," Audrey admitted weakly. "Snakes are more like it, though. I've got two snakes at table twenty."

Iris peeked out the door. "Regulars, aren't they? I think I've seen them here before." At Audrey's sullen nod, she added, "That blond one is a real looker, don't you think? He was at one of my tables a couple of weeks ago with his girlfriend. As a matter of fact, they asked to talk to you, as I recall."

"The woman he was with wasn't his—" Audrey swallowed her words. She certainly couldn't let on to Iris that she knew Brandon, or that she'd been foolish enough to socialize with an Angel Club patron outside work. She prided herself on her intelligence, and having fallen for Brandon was clear evidence of stupidity on her part. "Yes, he's the one."

"So? Fill me in," Iris requested.

"What's to fill in? He's a piece of slime, like all the others," Audrey snorted.

"Then how come you're shaking? One slime is like another," Iris observed philosophically.

"They're just obnoxious, that's all," Audrey explained. "They make my skin crawl."

"Take it easy," Iris consoled her. "Ignore it. Do your work and collect your tip." She appraised Audrey compassionately. "Wanna go out for coffee after we get off? You look like you need to unwind."

"I'd like that," Audrey accepted the invitation with a genuine smile. "Coffee after. If I survive."

"Survive," Iris ordered her. "I don't want to have to talk to a corpse at the diner. People might take me for a weirdo."

Audrey smiled crookedly and hoisted her tray. "The last thing I want is for anyone to take you for a weirdo, Iris," she assured her colleague as she followed her out of the kitchen.

As soon as she entered the dining room she felt Brandon's eyes upon her. His persistent stare seemed almost palpable, a tangible entity in the room's atmosphere, tracing her movements about the tables. It took all her self-control to remain poised and friendly with her other customers.

When she returned to Brandon's table to take their dinner orders, he accosted her almost at once. "Audrey," he murmured, apparently oblivious to his companion. "Audrey, this is serious. I have to see you after work tonight."

"You heard what I told your chum," she responded in a deceptively cool voice. "I've already got plans."

"I don't believe you," Brandon persevered.

The other man laughed. "I knew it, Fox, I knew it the last time we were here together." He winked at Audrey. "I'm afraid my buddy here has the hots for you in a big way, and I don't blame him one iota."

"His hots are not my problem," Audrey mumbled, aware that they were in fact very much her problem.

"See, Fox? If she's not available to me, why should she be available to you? You think you know women so well, but Audrey can tell you that you don't, can't you, sweetie?" He chuckled. "Maybe I can get her to testify for our side."

"Prager..." Brandon's voice held an unmistakable warning, but Prager only laughed again.

Despite the quivering of her fingers, Audrey managed to jot down their orders. She stalked to the kitchen and inhaled deeply to steady herself. Indeed, Brandon was no better than his companion. Just two despicable men coming on to her, competing for her as if she were a trophy. Brandon ought to count his blessings that she'd been suckered in by him once. He had some gall trying for seconds—especially at the club. He had even less sense than she'd given him credit for, chasing her here of all places. Unless, of course, it *was* just a competition for him, a game of one-upmanship he was playing with his pal.

She wondered if right now he was boasting to Prager that he'd already won the trophy once, that he'd outscored his rival for Audrey's attentions. The very thought made her nauseous. How could she have let him get to her?

She wasn't certain how she endured the remainder of the evening. Every time she had to approach Brandon's table her stomach clenched into a knot of fury and self-loathing for her stupidity in having trusted him. She recalled her decision last night not to use him in her study, and that only increased her distress. Brandon more than fit the profile of the typical girlie-club patron—he defined it. Like a pedigreed dog, he could easily be labeled "Best of Class." That was all he was, after all: a dog. With a fancy pedigree, perhaps—but just a slobbering dog.

Her anger didn't abate when Brandon left the restaurant, though it subsided to a slow burn that continued to agonize her throughout the evening. She was relieved when closing time finally arrived and she could drop her charming facade and get away from the restaurant, away from the place she associated with him.

She and Iris changed into their street clothes and headed out the staff exit leading to the parking lot. The moon was nearly full, and in its glowing light Audrey immediately noticed the silver Volvo parked near the driveway. Just like the first night she'd refused him, he had come back to see her.

Audrey gripped Iris's arm. "We'll take your car," she whispered hurriedly.

"What?"

Hearing the click of the Volvo's door opening, she tugged Iris across the lot to the dilapidated white Plymouth parked alongside Audrey's motorbike. "I'll come back for this later," she said, gesturing at the bike and anxiously waiting for Iris to unlock the car's passenger door. Hearing Brandon call out her name, she ducked into the car and slammed the door shut behind her, locking it with a forceful bang of her fist against the button.

"Isn't that the cute blond guy?" Iris asked innocently as she climbed in beside Audrey.

"Maybe he's blond, but by no stretch of the imagination is he cute," Audrey muttered. "Come on, let's get out of here. He gives me the willies."

Iris obediently started the engine and steered past the tall, frazzled-looking man who stood frowning in the center of the lot, staring at them.

Over coffee at the diner, Audrey remained evasive as Iris questioned her about Brandon. Just another customer, Audrey insisted. Just another lewd man, another little boy. Iris nodded compassionately and told Audrey about a similar experience she'd had several months ago with a persistent customer. "After a while he gave up," Iris consoled Audrey. "Men may be thick, but give them enough time and they catch on. You know how their egos are. Ignore them long enough and they go away."

Audrey contemplated Iris's words as they finished their coffee and drove back to the now empty parking lot of the restaurant. She continued to meditate as she rode home, undressed and crawled into bed. If only she'd been smart enough to ignore Brandon from the start, she remonstrated with herself. If only she'd trusted her instincts, if only she'd remembered the lessons of her past. She'd trusted her mentor in college, and he'd made a pass at her. She'd trusted her fellow graduate student, and he'd tried to sabotage her research. How many times would she make the same mistake? How many times would she let her emotions cloud her mind, allowing her to trust a man?

She awoke Friday poorly rested and disconsolate. Berating herself for having had faith in Brandon didn't make her feel any better. Knowing she'd been an idiot even to consider that she was in love with him only worsened her mood and sapped her self-confidence. As soon as she was dressed she located her written commentary on Brandon and added it to the manuscript insertions she'd be dropping off to Liz on campus. Brandon was the perfect sample for her profile on men and their inane tribal rituals, she decided.

She stuffed the papers into her briefcase along with her lecture notes and traveled to the university. The day was raw and chilly, and her bare hands were numb by the time she parked her bike. Forgetting to wear gloves was just one more bit of evidence of her stupidity, she thought as she raced to the nearest building and ducked inside. She made her way to her office through the heated underground maze of tunnels, pausing several times to blow on her hands and rub some feeling back into them.

Her morning lecture was disjointed owing to her distracted state, but she didn't care. After the class had officially ended, she was besieged by students who wanted to discuss their term papers with her, and she invited them back to her office when students for another class began to take seats in the classroom.

By the time she'd finished meeting with her anxious freshmen, it was well past one-thirty. Audrey didn't care about having missed lunch; she was too overwrought to eat anyway. But she did have to get her manuscript to Liz before her two o'clock class.

She grabbed her briefcase and left her office for the stairway. She jogged through the tunnels, deftly weaving among the surges of students, and she was out of breath when she reached the third floor of the Humanities building which housed Liz's office. She dashed down the corridor toward Liz's door.

As she slowed down to a stop it swung open, and out stepped Brandon. She stared at him in astonishment. What in heaven's name was he doing in Liz's office, of all places?

He seemed shocked to see Audrey too. Dressed in a business suit, toting an elegant leather attaché case, he stood motionless in the doorway, gazing at her. Her jaw went slack; her mouth grew parched. The muscles at the back of her throat seemed to become paralyzed, and she was unable even to swallow.

"Audrey, is that you?" Liz called out from her seat behind her cluttered desk.

"Uh-huh," she said falteringly, looking past Brandon.

"You wanted to drop that stuff off for me to read? Come on in—we're all done here."

Audrey turned back to Brandon, who nodded. "Yes, we're through," he assured her quietly. "You go in and talk to Dr. Simpson." He courteously stepped aside so she could enter the office.

Audrey opened her mouth and then shut it. She edged into the office and Brandon closed the door softly behind her. She stared at the solid black door for a moment, then spun around to Liz. "What was *he* doing here?"

Liz leaned back in her swivel chair and studied Audrey. "Do you know Brandon Fox?" she asked curiously.

"Better than I'd care to," Audrey muttered as she dropped limply onto a chair facing Liz.

"No kidding?" Liz's eyes lit up and her mouth stretched in a fascinated smile. "Want to explain?"

"He's a regular at the Angel Club."

"Brandon Fox?" Liz's eyebrows arched high. "An Angel Club regular? I don't believe you."

"Believe me or don't," Audrey grumbled. "It's the truth. What was he doing visiting you?"

"No, wait a minute," Liz demanded, obviously amazed. She shook her head incredulously. "The Angel Club? God. Never trust first impressions," she mused aloud. "I never would have pegged him as that type."

"Oh, he's more than the type," Audrey said bitterly. "He's the archetype. If you don't believe me, read this." She pulled her manuscript from her briefcase and dropped it onto Liz's desk. "It's all there. About the best thing I can say for Brandon Fox is that he's provided good material for my book. Why in the world was he here, Liz? If you're in the market for a lawyer, I'd recommend you keep looking."

Liz was rendered speechless. She spread open Audrey's folder and skimmed the top page, shaking her head. "I'm in shock," she confessed.

Audrey checked her watch and sighed. "Running late, as usual," she announced, standing. "Liz, we'll have to talk later. I've got a class to teach."

Liz glanced up from the folder as Audrey moved to the door. "Okay, later," she agreed. "But do me a favor and keep Tuesday lunchtime free, all right?"

"How come?" Audrey asked, swinging open the door.

"I'm organizing a rally at the Capital Club downtown for Tuesday at noon. A demonstration to protest their no-women policy. I want you there."

"Sure," Audrey promised. "Tuesday's a light day for me. Count me in." With that she swept out of the office.

She should have expected that Brandon would be waiting for her. He'd been leaning against the white cinder-block wall of the hallway, but he straightened up and pulled his hands from his pockets as soon as she emerged from Liz's office. "Audrey—"

"I can't talk," she said brusquely, starting down the hall to the stairway.

Brandon reached out and captured her arm, halting her. "We have to talk," he insisted.

The pressure of his hand against her flesh caused a warm current to spiral through her. As angry as she was with him, as much as she detested him, she couldn't deny the electric passion that sprang to life in her body whenever he touched her. Acknowledging his sensuality, his power over her, only made her despise him more. "We can't," she said breathlessly, struggling to fill her lungs with air. "I'm late for a class."

"We'll talk on the way," he resolved, accompanying her to the stairs. As they descended he said, "Audrey, it wasn't my choice to go to the Angel Club last night."

"Of course not," she snapped bitterly. "You had no say in the matter, I'm sure. Poor little Brandon, being forced to leer at the lovely ladies against his will."

"Audrey." He attempted to stop her, but she stubbornly continued down the stairs toward the basement level. Reluctantly he kept pace with her. "Audrey, I tried to phone you ahead of time to warn you that I'd be there. But you were never at home. Prager insisted that we meet there for dinner. It was just business."

"Right," she agreed cynically. "And what I do after hours is business too. Tell me about it." She furiously shoved open the door to the tunnel.

Brandon took a moment to adjust to the gloomy light of the underground corridor. "Where the hell are you taking me?" he asked as he surveyed the grungy walls, the exposed pipes and the forklift truck cruising past them.

"I'm not taking you anywhere," she retorted. "You're the one who's trying to take me. And yes, I did get taken, Fox. Go notch your belt—"

"Don't," he warned her, yanking her to a halt and twisting her to face him. "Audrey, please," he said more gently, his eyes glimmering with a troubled gray light. "Listen to me."

She drew in a breath and waited for him to speak.

"Audrey, I agreed to go to the Angel Club because...because Prager dared me. I know this may be hard for a woman to understand, but when a man gets dared in a certain way, it's almost like a reflex. He has to accept the dare. I'm dealing with him in a difficult case and if I didn't take him up on his challenge it might have made the negotiations more...I don't know." He sighed. "I want very badly to win this case, and I didn't think that fighting with him over where to eat dinner would help my side. Please try to understand."

He sounded so earnest and he looked so solemn that Audrey felt her anger weakening, overpowered by the desire to believe him. "Business, then," she mumbled warily. "In other words, your work makes you do things you don't like, just as mine does."

"Exactly," he agreed. His grip softened on her, though he didn't release her. "Last night wasn't important. The night we made love was. I know it was as important to you as it was to me. Don't let last night spoil everything between us."

"You think I should give you another chance?" she goaded him. "How many times does this make, I wonder?"

"Damn it, what do you want from me?" he exploded. "You've got my love, you've got my honesty—what more do you want? Should I jump through hoops of fire just to prove myself to you?"

The desire to believe him won out. She felt her body thawing, angling to his. Her head fell gently against his shoulder. "Brandon," she whispered tremulously. "I do want to trust you. I really do."

"Then you'll have to," he said, lifting his free hand to brush through the thick curls of her hair. She tilted her head back and his mouth sought hers.

He wasn't perfect, but no man was. Nor was any woman. Surely not Audrey herself. Brandon had given her his love and his honesty, the two most precious gifts any man could give a woman. She felt them in his kiss, in his embrace, in his helpless moan as her tongue discovered his. And no matter why he'd gone to the Angel Club last night, she loved him. Even her earlier disenchantment with him couldn't negate that fact.

"I love you too," she said softly, sliding her lips to his jaw.

His arms momentarily tightened on her, then relaxed. He kissed her brow and let go of her. "Go," he urged her, a pensive smile teasing his lips. "I don't want you to be late for your class. You've got a degree to earn, woman."

His command jolted her, and she hesitated. She had confessed her love to Brandon, but she still hadn't given him her honesty. "Brandon...we *do* have to talk," she insisted. "There are things I've got to tell you—"

"Not now," he prodded her. "Go to class. We'll talk when you've got time."

"I'm serious, Brandon. It's very important—"

"I'm sure it is. Maybe we can meet after you get off from work tonight," he suggested.

She shook her head. Eager as she was to finish her stint at the Angel Club, she'd scheduled after-work meetings with several other waitresses for every night of the weekend. "Not after work," she said. "I can't this weekend. I'm all booked up. Really."

Something hardened in his expression. "Every night?" She nodded.

"Do I dare to ask with whom?"

"Women," she assured him. "Waitresses. It's a long story, Brandon. I'll explain it when I can." She glimpsed her watch and gasped. Five minutes past two. "I've got to run. Monday night, maybe?"

"How about during the day tomorrow? Or Sunday?"

She thought about the nagging telephone call she'd had with her editor, and about the enormous amount of work still awaiting her on her manuscript if she was to get it into the mail by Monday afternoon. "The whole weekend's a mess," she said hurriedly. "I can't explain now, Brandon. I've really got to go. I'm incredibly late. Can we get together Monday evening? My schedule should be a bit calmer by then."

He shook his head. "Monday's no good for me. I've got another business dinner."

"The Angel Club's closed Mondays," Audrey remarked wryly. "I'm afraid to think where you might go for this one."

"This one's with my side," he clarified. "One of the senior partners and two of our clients. We'll go someplace reputable, I promise." He grazed her mouth with his. "Tuesday night and that's final."

"Tuesday night," she concurred. "I should be home in the afternoon. Call me then."

"I will," he promised, then nudged her down the hall. "Go. Don't miss your class. I hope I can find my way out of this maze," he added under his breath.

"Find a stairway and walk up a flight!" she hollered over her shoulder as she ran down the hall. "Tuesday night, Brandon—I'll explain everything then."

Her weekend passed in a blur. She worked at the Angel Club, went out for coffee afterward with a different waitress each night, and spent Saturday and Sunday afternoon hunched over her desk, toiling on her manuscript. She tried telephoning Liz several times, not only to get her feedback on the sections of the book, but to find out why Brandon had been at her office Friday—and to tell her that the excerpts concerning an anonymous patron of the club were once again null and void. But Liz's line was always busy, or else she wasn't home. Audrey realized that Liz must have her hands full with organizing her protest rally at the Capital Club.

Monday she got to see Liz, but they were both running late, and all Liz said as she tossed Audrey's folder onto her desk was, "It looks good—I penned in a few rephrasings and caught a couple of typos, but otherwise it looks fine. Is that stuff about Brandon Fox really true?"

"Yes and no," Audrey hedged. "Things are confusing between us, to say the least."

"I'm intrigued," Liz said with a chuckle. She hovered in Audrey's open office doorway, a stack of posters announcing the following day's demonstration in her hand. "I'm afraid I can't stick around to hear the details right now. Tomorrow you can tell me. Meet me at my office at eleven thirty, and we'll drive downtown to the rally together, okay?"

Audrey made a mental note of the appointed time. "Eleven thirty. I'll be there."

Her Tuesday morning seminar ran a few minutes past schedule, and Audrey stopped in her office only to drop off her briefcase and grab her jacket before heading for Liz's office. The day was sunny but the brisk wind was chilly, and Audrey knew she'd need her woollen jacket to keep warm while she stood outdoors on a street corner and listened to speeches. She'd participated in two other rallies Liz had organized, one for a local political candidate and one to demand better lighting on a residential street where a woman had been attacked. Liz always arranged for at least one dynamic speaker at such events.

Liz was locking up her office when Audrey arrived. "It's about time," she complained, tucking her brilliant red hair inside the collar of her blazer. She carried a battery-powered megaphone in one hand and two picket signs beneath her other arm. "I was about to come searching for you. Let's shake a leg. I'd hate to be late for my own rally."

Two other female professors met up with them on the first floor, and after stowing the picket signs in the trunk of her Chevy, Liz let the women in the car. "The trial against the Capital Club is scheduled to start Thursday," Liz explained. "But according to Mr. Fox, if he can pressure the club into settling out of court, all the better."

"Mr. Fox?" Audrey echoed in bewilderment. "Liz, what does Brandon have to do with all this?"

"He's representing the plaintiffs in the suit," Liz answered. "When I sent him the petition I wrote up in support of his clients, he contacted me to see what else I could do for him. Ergo, the rally."

Audrey mulled over Liz's revelation as the Chevy raced down Washington Avenue toward the business district on the eastern end of the city. Brandon represented the women who wanted to be admitted to a males-only club? Why should Audrey be surprised? He'd told her he was involved in civil rights litigation, and he'd sworn he believed in equality for women. It made perfect sense.

But what if he showed up at the rally? A demonstration wasn't the place for her to have to explain who she was and what she was up to at the Angel Club. How would she be able to justify her presence beside an associate professor of English without elaborating on her own professional situation?

Of course, students were likely to participate in the rally. Liz had posted announcements of the march all over campus, and Audrey was certain that some students would attend. But even so..."Is he going to be there?" she asked in a small voice. "Is Brandon Fox coming to this shindig?"

"He said he'd try to make it if he could," Liz replied. "What with the court date hanging over his head, he's probably got his hands full preparing his case, but he may make an appearance. Why? Would you like me to shout through the bullhorn that he's been known to spend his evenings at the Angel Club?"

"No!" Audrey replied emphatically. "Please don't do that, Liz. As I said, it's all very complicated." *And if there weren't two other women in the back seat I'd gladly fill you in,* she added silently. But she hardly knew those women, and she wasn't about to reveal her tumultuous emotional state to Liz in front of them.

For her emotions were in an uproar. After swearing that she'd never trust a man again, Audrey had broken her vow and chosen to trust Brandon. Her love required it, and she couldn't question the understanding that she loved him. She loved him enough to accept his reasons for being at the Angel Club three times in as many weeks, and to forgive him his blunders in dealing with her. For the first time in her life she was willing to love a man fully, flaws and all. She was willing to acknowledge that she'd been in error with him, that she'd jumped to the wrong conclusions about him, and that even his tendency to put his foot in his mouth around her couldn't lessen the affection she felt for him.

She loved him because he was decent and honest. She loved him because he could laugh about her falsified breasts—not only laugh about them but be relieved by her true dimensions. She loved him because he was brave enough to go against his background, his habits and his logic in pursuit of someone he thought was a cheap waitress, a woman unlike any he'd ever known before.

In turn, he was unlike any man she'd ever known before, and all she could do was match him in courage. Loving him went against her background and habits and logic as well. If he could be brave enough to take a chance on their love, so could she.

Several hundred women were already gathered around the wrought-iron entry gate of the Capital Club when Audrey and Liz arrived. The building was a charming brick Georgian several short blocks from the Empire State Mall, a modern complex of government and office buildings at the heart of the city's business district. Ever the anthropologist, Audrey surveyed the crowd with a professional eye. The vast majority were women, and while some were dressed casually a large number were attired for business. Evidently they were willing to commit their lunch hour to the demonstration. Audrey wondered how many of them wanted to join an old boys' association like the Capital Club. If anyone had a vested interest in seeing its doors opened to women, businesswomen did.

"There's Gilda Ramsey," Liz whispered to Audrey as she pointed out a smartly dressed woman standing with several similarly chic women at one side of the crowd. "A neighbor of mine, and one of the plaintiffs. She's the one who got me all worked up about this thing. A gutsy lady— you'd like her."

"Taking on the Capital Club isn't for the faint of heart," Audrey said with a grin.

"Well, Fox's law firm is known for winning cases like this," Liz intoned. "She's got the best ammo on her side. I wonder what she'd think if she knew her attorney spent his off-hours at the Angel Club."

"Please don't tell her," Audrey hastily requested. "He was there on business—negotiating with the opposing attorney, I think."

Liz eyed her curiously, but before she could speak she was approached by one of several policemen at the site. "Miss Simpson?" he began.

Liz bristled. "*Dr.* Simpson," she corrected him.

"Yes, well, someone pointed you out as one of the organizers here, ma'am, and I've got to tell you, more people showed up than we expected. They're blocking the street to traffic, and we can't have that. We didn't prepare for it. We haven't got sawhorses or anything..."

"What do you want me to do?" Liz asked with forced courtesy.

"Well, we thought maybe you could wave your signs here for a few minutes and then move up to the Mall. The plaza there is much more spacious, and you won't be disturbing the flow of traffic that way."

Liz pursed her lips, then sighed in concession. "Very well. We'll move on." She grabbed Audrey's shoulder and wove her way to the gate. She switched on her megaphone's amplifier, welcomed the demonstrators and announced the alteration in plans.

Audrey read a few of the placards as the group filed down the street toward the Mall: Business Clubs for Businesswomen! Open the Doors to All Qualified Human Beings! Women Belong in the Capital! She spied several reporters wielding cameras and grinned. Liz sure knew how to put a rally together with flair.

"Have you got some impassioned speaker lined up to inspire the troops?" she asked.

Liz nodded. "It's a surprise," she murmured cryptically. "You'll see when we get to the Mall."

Audrey prayed it wouldn't be Brandon. She couldn't locate him in the crowd. Despite its sprawling size, she knew that if he were present she'd be able to find him, and the fact that she didn't see him calmed her somewhat. Her arms began to swing more freely as she relaxed and felt the spirit of the rally infuse her.

At the Mall the crowd swarmed around the base of the Egg, a stark oval-shaped theater protruding from the paved plaza at one end of the Mall. Gripping Audrey's arm, Liz ascended to the top of the broad stairway leading to the Egg's front doors. She lifted her megaphone again.

"Ladies—and a few gentlemen," she addressed the crowd. "We all know why we're here today. The Capital Club, one of this city's oldest and most venerable social institutions, has discriminated against women since its inception, and the time to end that bigoted practice is long overdue. Several women have brought a class-action suit against the Capital Club to end this discrimination..." Liz identified her friend Gilda Ramsey and two of the women with her as plaintiffs in the suit. The crowd cheered and applauded.

"Well," Liz continued gustily, "we're very lucky today to have a speaker who knows more about all-male clubs, social and otherwise, than any of the rest of us. She's made the study of such clubs her profession, and perhaps she can enlighten us as to the behavior of men who participate in these societies and institutions. I'm kind of springing this on her as a surprise, but I think she'll be willing to share her knowledge with us." Liz winked at Audrey, who was beginning to feel very queasy. Liz lifted the megaphone to her mouth and announced, "Let me turn the spotlight over to her, then. Ladies—and gentlemen, you few courageous souls among us—please allow me to introduce Dr. Audrey Lambert of the state university's department of anthropology."

With that, she thrust the megaphone into Audrey's hands and stepped aside.

Eight

Brandon felt silly chasing down the street after a massive throng of chanting women. He'd arrived late for the rally at the Capital Club, and a police officer explained to him that owing to its size the demonstration was being moved to the Empire State Mall. Brandon had to run to catch up with the crowd.

He almost hadn't come to the rally at all. Thornton had expressed mixed sentiments about such a ploy over dinner last night and again this morning. "If Prager thinks we're behind this protest rally, he's going to view it as an indication that our case is so weak we've got to rely on street theater to make our point," he'd criticized.

"But we *aren't* behind the rally," Brandon had maintained. "The entire thing is the brainchild of Dr. Simpson at the university. All I did was tell her I didn't disapprove." He'd managed to keep his tone level and dispassionate, though he couldn't resist a twinge of frustration with Thornton. The senior partner's thoughts were sound, but he was a bit old-fashioned when it came to tactics. He firmly trusted that justice could be reached through the standard procedures of a court trial. Brandon was younger; he'd come of age during the time in his nation's history when people believed that a war could be ended or a corrupt president unseated if enough bodies took to the streets. Like Thornton, Brandon had faith in judicial processes—he wouldn't have become a lawyer if he hadn't had that faith. But he was open-minded enough to allow room for alternative strategies.

The group of protesters congregated about the base of the Egg, and Brandon surveyed the crowd, looking for his clients. When Liz Simpson pointed out Gilda Ramsey and Josephine Stork, Brandon smiled and circled the mob to stand by them.

He turned his attention back to Liz as she introduced a new speaker, and his mouth dropped open. "...Dr. Audrey Lambert of the state university's department of anthropology," Liz announced, and suddenly there was Audrey, *his* Audrey, Audrey the struggling student, the Angel Club waitress, taking the megaphone from Liz.

Audrey. *Dr. Audrey Lambert*. Specialist in studies of male-oriented societies. Brandon couldn't believe it.

But now she was speaking, her sweet soft voice only slightly distorted by the megaphone's amplifier. "Liz told me that today's speaker would be a surprise for me," she began, "and I'm afraid it is. I haven't got a prepared speech, so I'll have to wing it." She was dressed in a brown wool jacket and tailored tan slacks. The wind lifted the silky black curls covering her head, creating a halo more naturally beautiful than that cockeyed silver hoop she wore pinned to her hair at the Angel Club.

"My research has taken me to unlikely places," she continued. "I've never been inside the Capital Club—"

"No woman ever has!" someone shouted from the crowd. The comment was greeted by loud hoots and hisses.

Audrey smiled, her dark gaze drifting about the throng to locate the speaker. "To be honest with you, I'm much more familiar with another of Albany's male-oriented clubs, the Angel Club, just south of here on Pearl Street. The Angel Club, the center of my current research, is what I call a 'girlie joint.' Waitresses dress in deliberately seductive outfits and pander to the fantasies of male customers. Just as at the Capital Club, men discuss business at the Angel Club, but their attitude toward women is more overtly expressed. The men who habituate such clubs long to escape from the reality of women. They don't wish to view women as their equals, as their rivals in business, or as their partners in society. Instead they see women as playthings, sex objects, creatures designed for the sole purpose of catering to their male prerogatives. At the Angel Club, women are not supposed to reveal their brains— they're only supposed to smile prettily and display their physical assets. They're viewed as little more than prostitutes by their male customers, and that's the myth all-male clubs like to perpetuate.

"I'm sure the Capital Club isn't filled with sexy waitresses, but the purpose of the Capital Club is no different from that of the Angel Club—to perpetuate the myth that men are superior to women, and that women are put on this earth not to deal in commerce and law, not to govern this city or this state, not to participate fully in the business of civilization, but simply to bear children or to satisfy men's primal urges. Not all men view women this way, as those of you men present can testify," she hastily added, her eyes once again skimming the crowd, picking out the scattered men in the group. As her vision shifted to her right she spied Brandon and flinched.

Their gazes locked. She looked fearful to him, and somewhat apologetic. He could only guess how he looked to her: shocked, dumbfounded. Enraged.

Research. So that was what she was up to—research. His brain flipped through a high-speed flashback of their entire relationship. He recalled Audrey's innate intelligence, her eloquent vocabulary, her ability at bridge, the many signs she'd given him of her educated background. He recalled her indignation every time he implied that she was in any way inferior to him. He recalled his own troubling attraction to her, his bewilderment that he could have been so taken by a woman's appearance rather than her mind.

Yet maybe he *had* been attracted to her mind. Dr. Lambert, a university professor—she wasn't so terribly unlike the women he was generally interested in, after all.

Don't kid yourself, Fox, he grumbled. In Audrey's case it *had* been her appearance that had drawn him in. It *had* been her Angel Club persona that had captivated him. From the start Audrey had tapped into his secret, subliminal yearnings. She'd uncovered the male animal that lurked beneath his proper, respectful facade. His first impression of her was that she was a temptress, and that was the impression he'd acted on.

And what was he to her? Just another example in her research. Just another test subject, another man who proved her thesis about all men.

Yet he wasn't like that. He'd tried to convince her that he wasn't, and at times he was sure he had nearly persuaded her. But she'd resisted him, trying again and again to make him fit her research.

He felt tricked. He felt betrayed. He felt bamboozled.

He loved Audrey. Now he was learning that he didn't even know who she was. He hadn't known until this very moment that she was exactly the woman he was looking for: both a brilliant scholar and a sexy lady. Or, as she might contemptuously express it: a madonna and a whore rolled into one.

He loved, and she was only using him. She was exploiting him as evidence, as an illustration to make a scientific point. Her claim last Friday that she loved him too wasn't enough for Brandon. It was too little, too late. Now that she'd gotten what she wanted from him—a few more scraps of proof for her scholarly study—she could say whatever she wanted to him. Her words of love couldn't change the fact that she'd been dishonest with him from the start, that she'd misrepresented herself to him in order to analyze him for her damned research.

A hard, cold lump of bitterness lodged in his chest, making it difficult for him to breathe. He'd never felt so abused in his life.

She spoke for only a few more minutes, her voice subdued and her eyes concertedly avoiding his. Then she passed the megaphone back to Liz Simpson and tripped down the stairs, working her way through the mob toward him.

Brandon steeled himself for her approach. His mind didn't register Liz's concluding statement about the impending trial, about how even with the Capital Club's case entering the courts she wanted those present to remain fired up for the cause until the plaintiffs won and the doors open to all qualified members. All he could think about was Audrey's deception.

She reached him as the crowd began to disperse. "Brandon..." she murmured.

Shoving his hands into his pockets, he nodded grimly.

"Brandon—I wanted to tell you. I know now isn't the right time or the right place, but I told you I had to explain and—"

"I don't want to hear about it," he said softly. "You're a liar, Audrey. A phony and fake."

Her eyes misted over, and she dropped her gaze to the stretch of concrete separating their feet. "I'm a researcher," she said, defending herself. "I do what I have to do to gather information. Given that my specialty is male tribal rituals in America, I sometimes have to go undercover to learn things. That doesn't make me a phony."

"Oh, it doesn't?" he snorted. "And what important things did you learn in bed with me? Was that a good research experience for you?"

She didn't speak for a moment. "Yes," she admitted meekly. "Sometimes research demonstrates the exact opposite of what one is trying to prove, and the researcher has to readjust her thinking. So yes, Brandon, I learned something important."

"I'm glad I could be of assistance," he snapped. "Now, if you've gotten everything you want from me, I've got to get back to my office."

He turned from her and took one step before she grabbed his arm. "Brandon," she pleaded, addressing his back when he wouldn't face her. "Brandon, I admit I was wrong about you, but honestly, I wasn't completely wrong. When we first met, you thought the same things about me as most men who go to the Angel Club think about the women who work there. You didn't love me then. You only lusted for me, and you know it."

He shuddered. The truth in her accusation cut to the bone. "And you?" he countered, spinning around to confront her. "Did you approach me as a human being or as an anthropological specimen? Did you think of me as a person or as someone designed to perpetuate your myths about men?''

"At least I wasn't looking at you as a sex object," she commented.

He snorted. "Oh? How about when we made love, Audrey? How about then? You were still playing games with me then, weren't you? I still didn't know the truth about you, but you went right ahead and let me make love to a masquerade, to a fake, a—a total stranger."

"Brandon—I wanted to tell you that night. I unstuffed my bra and rehearsed my speech and...oh, Brandon, I tried to tell you!"

"But you didn't."

"Because..." She swallowed, her hand softening on his arm. "Because whenever you touch me I can't even think," she confessed timorously.

He painstakingly removed her fingers from his sleeve. "Then by all means, we'd better not touch anymore," he said. "Far be it from me to want to keep a smart woman like you from thinking." He cast her a final, scathing glare, then spun around and stalked resolutely across the plaza toward the street.

His muscles were still clenched in anger when he returned to his office and shut himself inside. Like Audrey, he couldn't think when she touched him, even when her touch wasn't physical. She was still touching him emotionally, spiritually. And he couldn't think.

All he could do was feel. His emotions stumbled over themselves, a swirling tangle of hurt, resentment, remorse. The worst of it wasn't that she'd been wrong about him but that she'd been right in many ways. Her deception had exposed his imperfections, and he didn't know how to cope with them. He *had* lusted after her, long before he realized that he loved her. He wanted to believe that he was righteous and responsible, that love always preceded desire in his dealings with women—that lust had nothing to do with it at all. But Audrey had bared the truth about him in a way that left him severely shaken.

It was easier to be angry with her than with himself, but if he was going to face up to the truth he had to acknowledge that his self-image was as much a deception as her behavior with him had been. He had always spoken the right line when it came to women's equality, but knowing Audrey had rendered his pious declarations about women meaningless. He'd approached her thinking that she was merely a tawdry waitress with big breasts, and he'd wanted her. Completely ignorant about her knowledge and intelligence, he'd wanted her more than he'd ever wanted a woman before.

The ringing of the telephone jarred him from his ruminations, and he lifted the receiver. "Mr. Prager is on the line for you," the secretary announced.

"Fine," Brandon responded limply. "Put him through."

"Fox?" Prager bellowed. "Jesus, why didn't you tell me they were going to be storming the Bastille?"

"There were signs posted around town proclaiming the demonstration," Brandon replied wryly. "I didn't know you wanted a personalized invitation."

"Invitation? Come on, Fox, give me the scoop. Are you going to be importing a horde of harpies waving picket signs into the courtroom every day?"

"I didn't organize the rally," Brandon insisted. "I okayed it, but it was organized by a woman who teaches at the university. In court I plan to rely on valid legal arguments."

"Who knows if we'll get to court?" Prager groaned. "Listen, man, my people are humiliated. They're trembling in their boots. Good lord, there were reporters at that rally. Television reporters. This thing's going to make the six o'clock news.''

"Probably," Brandon allowed nonchalantly.

"All right." Prager sighed. "I've got a two thirty meeting at the club to talk things over with the board. Maybe we can work out an accommodation. Are you interested?"

"I've been interested from the start," Brandon answered. "Talk to them and see what you can work out. You understand, of course, that we're discussing monetary damages as well as a new membership policy."

"Don't lecture me on my own business," Pragar grumbled. "I've read the suit. I'm not making any promises, but this stupid demonstration may just nudge us into a breakthrough. Let me meet with my people and see where they want to take this thing."

"Fair enough. Should we get together afterward?"

"Right. I should be at the Capital Club till around four thirty. Why don't you come around to the club then and we'll chew over what we've got."

"I'll be there," Brandon promised before hanging up.

He stared at his telephone for several minutes, wondering whether he should call his clients and inform them that a settlement was imminent. He decided against it. Such an announcement might be premature. It was possible that once the Capital Club's board of directors stopped trembling in their boots they might decide to dig in their heels, to fight their case to the last man if necessary. Brandon would wait until he talked to Prager later that afternoon before making any triumphant declarations.

A light rap on his door preceded Karen's voice. "Bran? Can I come in?"

"Sure," he called out.

Karen stepped into his office, carrying a folder, and swooped toward his desk. "How'd it go?" she asked. "Did you make it to the rally?"

Brandon nodded, mulling over whether to inform Karen about Audrey's appearance at the rally. He decided not to. He was still too hurt, too insulted and angry and bewildered, to try to put his feelings into words. Instead, he reported, "I just got off the phone with Prager. His people are running scared. The odds are improving for an out-of-court settlement."

"Wonderful!" Karen cheered. "Congrats, Bran. That's terrific!"

"Don't jump the gun," he cautioned Karen. "Nothing's settled yet. Prager's going to meet with his people in a couple of hours, and then I'm heading over to the Capital Club at four thirty to see what we can hammer out. They haven't waved the white flag yet."

"They will," Karen predicted. "And then you can assist me on my new case: William Pankston. Did Thornton mention anything to you about it?"

Brandon shook his head and fidgeted with a pen.

"He's a history teacher at one of the high schools in Troy. Dismissed—told this was his last term teaching and he's got to go. He claims it's because of his anarchist politics."

"Does he preach anarchism in class?" Brandon asked, mildly interested.

"He says he doesn't," Karen answered. "I think he's got a good case. Wanna sign on?"

"Let me see how the Capital Club situation progresses," Brandon demurred. "If we do go to trial, I'm going to have my hands full."

Karen accepted his maybe. "Well, here's Pankston's file to thumb through," she said, tossing the folder onto

Brandon's blotter. "Isn't it just typical of the way things are run around here that a white male Protestant gets to argue a case for women, and a woman gets to argue a case for a white male Protestant?"

"I hate to say it, Karen, but it does make sense. Juries are a strange breed; they react to different lawyers in different ways. I don't have to tell you that."

With a nod of agreement, Karen stood and walked to the door. "Give it a read and let me know what you think," she requested. "You can drop it off on your way to the Capital Club. I guess it's just as well you're on that case," she concluded. "They'd never let *me* through the door to meet Prager there." With that she was gone.

Brandon opened the folder. He had difficulty concentrating on the neatly typed brief and the background information Karen had accumulated. Maybe Karen wondered about the logic that led her to represent a man in court while Brandon represented women, but it made perfect sense to him.

Instead he wondered about his own case. He wondered about Prager's call. He wondered about Audrey. Especially about Audrey.

Shoving the folder away, he turned his attention fully to her and gave in to his feelings. He wondered whether his resentment about her treatment of him was like the resentment women had when they were misled by men. He wondered how many times men had misrepresented themselves to women in order to seduce them, how many times a beautiful woman like Audrey was treated like a piece of meat instead of like a person with a mind and a spirit. He wondered once again about her background, about the agonizing lessons she'd learned watching her father deceive her mother. He wondered why women hadn't risen up in protest centuries ago.

He really couldn't blame women for their resentment. He couldn't blame Karen for hating her in-laws, who wanted her to be a meek, dependent wife, or for lashing back at Tim when he made disparaging comments about women, even in jest. He couldn't blame women, because now, more than ever, he understood what they went through in their relationships with men. Before he'd met Audrey, his understanding was only theoretical, but now he was living through it, and his understanding was painfully real.

He resented her. He was hurt. And yet he understood her too.

At a quarter after four he packed up his papers and straightened out his desk. He latched his attaché case shut and left his office, dropping off Karen's folder before he headed for the Capital Club. He tried to imagine what the Club's board of directors had told Prager that afternoon. He tried to put himself inside their skulls, to predict their reactions to the noontime demonstration. Undoubtedly they'd spent an hour squawking about their rights to privacy, their club's heritage as an all-male preserve, their rationalizations of the status quo.

Then, after registering their indignation, perhaps they'd silenced themselves and listened to Prager's advice: drop the case. Settle out of court. Give up. Brandon found Prager personally abhorrent, but he was a shrewd lawyer. He knew how to read the signs. The Capital Club was bound to lose its case in court, and as an attorney it was Prager's job to advise his clients to cut their losses and concede.

The staid brick building housing the club appeared untouched by the day's events. Brandon noticed that there were no vans from the television news bureaus in the club's parking lot, although reporters might already have come

and gone. He strode to the front door and hurried inside
the entry vestibule, glad to be out of the late afternoon's
cold wind.

An imposing butler in formal attire stood guard at the
inner door. "May I help you?" he asked, giving Brandon
an imperious perusal.

"I'm supposed to meet John Prager here at four thirty,"
said Brandon.

"Please wait here," the butler ordered him before van-
ishing through the door. Brandon waited alone, studying
the intricate mosaic pattern of the floor's tiles and trying
to clear his mind of everything but the business at hand.

The butler returned shortly and beckoned Brandon inside the inner doors. They swept through an enormous
high-ceilinged sitting room, elegantly decorated with heavy
leather wing-back chairs, polished mahogany side tables,
and a large marble fireplace set in one wall with a fire
crackling on the hearth. As the butler led him across the
plush carpeting, Brandon scanned the room. An elderly
man dozed in an easy chair, a teacup and saucer set on the
table beside him. Several other men were engrossed in
copies of *The Wall Street Journal, Barron's,* and the local
papers. At one felt-covered card table three men were absorbed in a game of pinochle, and at another two men bent
over a blueprint, analyzing the architectural design before
them.

The butler escorted Brandon through an arched doorway into a back hall and down it to an open door. From
the doorway Brandon peered into a paneled conference
room. Six men, one of them Prager, were seated about the
elongated table. At Brandon's entrance Prager stood.
"Gentlemen, the enemy has arrived," he announced.

Brandon nodded a greeting to Prager and then examined the faces of the other men. They didn't appear re-

signed in the least, he noticed. He turned to Prager and asked, "Well? Have your people come to a decision?"

"My people," Prager spoke on the men's behalf, "seem to feel that one showy display of theatrics does not a suit decide. Is that right, boys?"

"I'm afraid so," said one of the older men at the table, fussing nervously with his necktie. "I think, Mr. Fox, that we're going to have to settle this issue in court."

"I see," Brandon said thoughtfully. "I assume you understand that a court trial is going to run into a great expense and you're going to lose anyway."

The men chuckled tolerantly. "I'm sure your lovely ladies pay you to say that, Mr. Fox," one of them said. "But it isn't true."

"Time will tell," Brandon granted. "Prager, maybe you and I should retire for some private discussion."

Prager shuffled his papers into a tidy stack and stuffed them into his briefcase. "I'm all done here, I suppose— unless you want to use one of the smaller rooms upstairs. We can have a couple of drinks while we talk in the comfort of this fine bastion of gentlemanly propriety." His wink when he described the Capital Club gave Brandon a small measure of hope that he and Prager might still reach an out-of-court agreement.

Before he could speak, the butler who guarded the club's front door reappeared at the doorway of the conference room. He cleared his throat loudly, and the men turned to him. "Excuse me, gentlemen," he intoned. "There's a woman at the front door to see Mr. Prager."

"A woman here?" the oldest man at the table reiterated. "Hopkins, you know we don't allow women inside, other than the cleaning and cooking staff."

"Well, yes, but..." The butler hesitated. "Perhaps I shouldn't have referred to her as a woman. She's more of a...er...a lady." He assessed the curious stares that met him before elaborating. "She says her name is Audrey, and she's a friend of Mr. Prager's from the Angel Club. She has stopped by on her way to work. She says he extended to her an invitation to squeeze him in whenever she could." Clearly these last few words caused the stodgy butler some discomfort, because his cheeks colored slightly as he repeated them.

Brandon's brow tensed in a frown. What was Audrey doing here? Why was she claiming that she still worked at the Angel Club, and what did she want with Prager, of all people?

The other men in the conference room reacted with bawdy comments. One whistled. Prager took their teasing in stride. "My friends," he declared, "Audrey from the Angel Club is definitely not a woman. She's an angel, and I don't believe there's any club rule against allowing angels entry. I think we ought to let her in. You'll thank me once you get a good look at her."

Several men harrumphed, but the talkative older man laughed. "You make her sound so tempting, I'm almost willing to bend the rules in this case."

"I'll meet her out in the main sitting room," Prager declared. "Let me just see what she wants."

The butler nodded. "She *is* dressed rather...flimsily," he tactfully stated. "And it's quite chilly outside. I'll show her into the sitting room."

As soon as the butler departed the rest of the men stood and joined Brandon at the door. Prager nudged him in the ribs. "What did I tell you, Fox?" he snickered. "The girl definitely has taste when it comes to men."

Brandon could think of nothing to say in response. His thoughts zigzagged wildly through his brain, and he struggled to order them and compose himself before he had to see Audrey. *What the hell is she doing?* he thought furiously. *What the hell is she up to now? More research? More exploitation of men? What in the name of God...?*

The men arrived en masse in the sitting room to discover Audrey standing by the fireplace, warming herself. Her eyes and lips were slathered with makeup, and her lined trench coat was unbuttoned to reveal her skimpy waitress uniform, complete with the stiletto-heeled shoes, the dark lacy stockings, the artificially huge dimensions of her bustline straining the décolletage of her silver leotard. It took all of Brandon's willpower not to shout that she should remove her damned socks and stop trying to trick men into making fools of themselves.

The other men in the sitting room were clearly astonished by her stunning presence. The card game had stopped, the architects were ignoring their blueprint, and even the dozing gray-haired tea drinker was wide awake and staring appreciatively at the woman by the fireplace.

Audrey smiled at Brandon, evidently not at all surprised to see him. She turned her smile to Prager and sidled up to him, her hips shifting sensuously as she tottered on her high heels. "Hello, Prager," she cooed. "Thanks so much for letting me inside."

Prager immediately slid his arm around her narrow waist. "You know I can't resist you, Audrey," he said with a leering smirk. "Friends, what did I tell you? Is this a woman or is this an angel?"

The members of the club's board remained silent. They were too busy ogling Audrey to speak. Brandon stifled the urge to tell them to put their bulging eyes back into their heads or he'd do it for them. How dare they gawk at *his* Audrey that way?

Audrey didn't seem perturbed by their stares, or by Prager's arm around her. She tilted her head back to gaze into his eyes. "Mr. Prager, I was just dying to see you," she purred. "After today, you see, when I heard about that silly little march downtown to protest what's going on here at the club, well, I just couldn't believe it. I simply had to see it for myself."

"See what, sweetheart?" Prager asked.

"This club, of course. Why, I just couldn't believe that women weren't allowed in here. It seemed so absolutely absurd that a group of men like you wouldn't want to be surrounded by women the way you like to be surrounded by women at the Angel Club." She discreetly slipped out of Prager's clutch to circulate among the other men in the room. "Why, men just love having an attractive woman to look at every now and then, don't they? I mean, isn't it more interesting than reading *Barron's*?" she asked the man whose copy of the business journal had fallen unnoticed to the floor as he gaped longingly at her. She bowed from the waist to pick it up for him, offering him an enticing glimpse of her cleavage. "Here, sir. Surely you didn't mean to drop this, did you?"

"Thank you," he whispered eagerly. Brandon fumed at her wanton display. Did she realize that the man was thanking her not for retrieving his journal but for providing him with a close look at her bosom?

"A few women like Audrey might brighten this place up some," one of the board members conceded with a boyish grin.

Overhearing him, Audrey flashed him a pert smile before sauntering over to the table where the architects sat. "And what's this? A blueprint? How interesting," she said. "I think you should put a window here," she said, pointing at the blueprint. She didn't give the architects a chance to speak before wandering to two men seated on a leather sofa with a stack of papers spread across their knees. "And these must be contracts. Fascinating, the things you men do in a fine club like this." Her smile fading, she strolled directly to Brandon's side. "Mr. Fox? I'd be happy to testify for you in court. Obviously business *is* conducted in this presumably private social club, and even more obviously, a woman can enter, but only if she isn't wearing a business suit. Please feel free to subpoena me. You can contact me in care of the university's department of anthropology." With brisk nod, she glided directly to the door.

Prager's smirk dissolved into a grimace as he turned on Brandon. "What are you up to, Fox?"

Brandon's jaw moved up and down as he tried to fathom what had just occurred. "I'll—uh—I'll be in touch with you," he said quickly. "Good day, gentlemen."

With that, he turned and ran after Audrey.

Nine

She heard his loping gait along the building's front walk as he chased her, and she realized that nothing was to be gained in trying to outrun him. Instead she drew to a halt at the gate and fastened shut her trench coat, turning up the collar about her exposed throat. The sun had set, taking with it the last of the day's warmth. Despite her coat's wool lining, she was freezing in her scant uniform.

His hand fell heavily onto her shoulder. "Would you mind explaining what that was all about?" he growled.

She sucked in a deep breath, but the air was so raw her lungs seemed to freeze for an instant. She quickly exhaled and turned to him. "I thought it would be helpful to you," she said. "Obviously women *are* admitted into the Capital Club if they're dressed for the occasion."

"Come on, Audrey—be honest with me for once in your life."

"I *am* being honest," she argued. "No matter what you think of me, I'm on your side in this lawsuit, and I figured I'd do whatever I could for you. Marching down the street to the Mall might not have been enough. In case you haven't figured it out, Fox, I happen to be adept at disguising myself in a costume and weaseling my way into places women like me usually don't go. It's a part of my job as an anthropologist. If Margaret Mead could live with the Samoans in order to study their culture, why can't I visit the culture centers I want to study?"

Brandon weighed her answer and frowned. "So you just decided on a whim to visit the Capital Club?"

"It wasn't a whim," Audrey contended, lowering her eyes from his. They looked so angry, so distrustful, a harsh, icy gray. She sighed. "You were supposed to phone me this afternoon," she reminded him.

Her comment took him aback, and his frown deepened. "After what happened at the rally, I thought all bets were off."

She nodded, having expected such a response. She dug her hands into her pockets, trying futilely to warm them. "I phoned you instead," she revealed. "I got the name of your firm from Liz and called you there, but you had already left. So I asked to speak to Karen. She told me where you'd gone, and why. When she said Prager would be there too, I figured I'd try to get through the door and take a look around."

"But you asked for Prager, not for me," Brandon pointed out, his tone laced with confusion.

"Of course. If I asked for you, do you think I'd have been allowed inside? I have a good idea of the way Prager's mind works. He's the one who fits perfectly into my research. He's the kind of man I understand. So I asked for him." A gust of frigid wind blasted over them, and she shivered and hugged her coat more snugly about her body.

"You're going to catch your death out here, dressed the way you are," Brandon muttered. His concern for her well-being touched her, though she didn't dare to take it as a sign of forgiveness on his part.

"Then I'd better get myself home," she conceded reluctantly. Perhaps now wasn't the time to straighten things out with Brandon. He still seemed too furious with her to listen to reason. Maybe she shouldn't have invaded the Capital Club. While her action hadn't exactly been impulsive, her hope that it would somehow soften him to her probably was.

He scanned the parking lot. "Where's your motorcycle?"

"I took the bus here," she informed him. "I couldn't ride my bike dressed like this."

He curled his fingers around her elbow and ushered her to his Volvo. "I'll take you home," he offered gruffly.

Once they were in the car, he started the engine and steered north. "This isn't the right direction," Audrey protested.

"We're going to my place," he returned, his tone dispassionate. "We did have a date for this evening."

"But—" She floundered. When Brandon had failed to call her that afternoon, she'd assumed that—as he himself had said—all bets were off. "I'm not dressed to go out."

"Then we'll stay in. We've got some talking to do," he said evenly.

He drove to a pretty tree-lined block of genteel brownstones and parked. They entered one of the well-maintained townhouses and climbed to the second floor, where Brandon unlocked the door to his apartment. In the entry foyer Audrey unbuttoned her coat and shivered again. She rubbed her hands briskly together. "Can you turn up the heat or something? I'm really freezing."

"You ought to wear gloves outside," he admonished her, strolling to the thermostat and clicking it on. Then he took her coat from her and hung it in a closet. "Winter comes early to Albany, in case you haven't noticed." His voice sounded slightly gentler when he asked, "How about a drink?"

Audrey nodded. "Something hot," she requested. "I've got to thaw out."

He eyed her flimsy uniform and smiled enigmatically. She followed him into a spacious kitchen and took the seat he offered her on one of two teak stools next to a butcherblock island at the center of the room. A rack of copper-bottomed pots hung from the ceiling above the island, and the rest of the room bore further evidence that Brandon was a well-equipped amateur chef. He had an oversized refrigerator, a two-oven gas range, a double-basin sink, and an assortment of modern appliances arranged neatly on the counters. Audrey recalled the fresh-baked bread he'd served at their picnic and winced regretfully as she remembered her skepticism about his claim that he'd baked the bread himself.

He moved directly to a counter and filled an electric grinder with coffee beans. Pulverizing them released their rich fragrance into the room; the aroma alone seemed to warm her. He set up his coffeemaker, and while it brewed he fetched a bottle of Irish whiskey, a sugar bowl, a container of cream and two tall mugs.

Audrey pulled off her uncomfortable shoes and wiggled her toes. She groaned at the throbbing in her lower back. "Have you got a bathroom?" she asked. "I'd like to wash off this makeup."

His expression still unreadable, he gestured toward the hall. "Second door on the left," he directed her.

She padded down the hall to the bathroom and shut herself inside. The two vertical fluorescent lights lining the mirror above the sink glared when she turned them on, and she screwed her face into a grimace as she inspected the overlay of cosmetics on her features. As she smeared the lipstick from her mouth, she heard a telephone ring, and then Brandon's footsteps down the hall past the bathroom. The ringing stopped.

She scrubbed off her mascara and eyeliner, managing to keep the soap out of her eyes, and then plucked her socks from the front of her uniform. She studied her reflection intently. She wanted to look beautiful for Brandon; she wanted to look her best when she revealed her soul to him. She wanted him to believe her, to regain his trust in her and to accept her apology for having deceived him.

But she didn't think she looked beautiful at all. Her eyes appeared teary, and her lips refused to curve in a smile. At least without the face paint she looked honest, she thought as she appraised her image. Looking honest, looking like the person she actually was, was the most important thing right now.

Leaving the bathroom, she heard his muffled voice emerging from behind a closed door. Not wishing to eavesdrop, she went back to the kitchen and resumed her seat by the butcherblock table.

After a few minutes Brandon joined her. His jacket and tie were removed, his sleeves cuffed to the elbows. He strode directly to the counter to finish preparing the Irish coffee. "I hope you don't mind that I'm not whipping the cream," he said.

"Of course not."

He stirred the ingredients in the two mugs and carried them to the butcherblock table, then took his seat on the stool beside hers. "That was Prager," he said with a nod in the direction of the telephone. "The Capital Club has decided to settle out of court."

"Because of what I did?" Audrey asked.

Brandon nodded again before tasting his drink.

Audrey sipped hers as well. It warmed her mouth and chest, the kick of the whiskey seeping into her veins and reaching her strained muscles. She lowered her mug and studied Brandon. "You don't seem terribly pleased," she observed.

"I am," he insisted, his smile oddly wistful. "It's usually a good idea to reach a settlement without dragging a case through the courts. It's cheaper and more expedient, anyway."

"But...?"

"But," he admitted with a sigh, "I guess I would have preferred that the club had reached its decision not because they were humiliated by your antics and scared about your threat to testify against them, but because they respected the principles at issue in the case."

Audrey ran a slender finger pensively along the handle of her mug. "Principles are fine, Brandon," she commented softly. "But sometimes they get in the way of the truth. They can blind you to reality."

"Oh?" He angled his head, curious to hear more.

"I don't doubt my principles, Brandon," Audrey declared hesitantly. "They were shaped by experience, and they've guided me through some difficult times. But they kept getting in the way when it came to you, Brandon. Suddenly they don't seem very helpful." She lapsed into silence, gnawing her lower lip and trying to organize her thoughts.

"I'm listening," he urged her to go on.

She swallowed. "My instincts tell me that I shouldn't trust men. They tell me that men are hypocrites and cheaters. Every man I ever opened my heart to ended up failing me. In graduate school..." She paused to reminisce, her gaze fastened to the creamy surface of her drink. "In graduate school the man I thought I was in love with was so jealous of my professional success that he destroyed some of my notes for my thesis. Fortunately I had copies, so he didn't do much damage. To my research, that is," she added wryly. She took a deep breath, then continued. "In college my favorite professor, a man I worshipped, a man so brilliant and talented that I decided to become an anthropologist just to emulate him—he tried to seduce me, Brandon, and when I refused to give him what he wanted, he lowered my grade."

"You should have brought a suit against him," Brandon interjected indignantly. "That's against the law."

"You're a lawyer," she granted with a bitter chuckle. "Of course you'd suggest that. But I was already a senior, all set to go on to the University of Wisconsin for graduate school. I didn't have the time or the money to fight it out. It was easier just to leave and get on with my life. More expedient," she added with an ironic sniff.

Brandon grunted in assent.

"And of course there was my father," she concluded, with a sigh. "The first man in my life. I adored him, Brandon, the way any daughter adores her father. I know he didn't love me the way I loved him—he wanted a son, not a daughter. But I still loved him. I thought he was perfect. Then I grew up and learned the truth. He was a philanderer. A tyrant. Selfish and mule-headed." she curled her lip distastefully. "A typical man."

Brandon opened his mouth to refute her, but she cut him off before he could speak. "That's where my principles come from, Brandon. That's what formed my view of men. It's more comforting to stick to them sometimes than to revise your views. Just as it's simpler to study cultures than individuals. But doing that distorts the truth, and it leads to misconceptions. I didn't want to believe the truth about you, Brandon, because I was afraid to lose the values that structured my thinking, that got me through life." Again she sensed that he was about to protest, and she stifled him by announcing, "You did the same thing with me, Brandon, and you know it. Loving me went against everything you believed or expected from yourself."

"Not really," he argued. "As it turns out, you're just the sort of woman I value most. Smart, educated, professional...it's not as if you're a typical waitress—"

"But I *am*," she asserted emphatically. "At least I was. I think I'm ready to quit my job at the Angel Club—I've gotten all the information I need from working there." She turned fully to him. "But until I hand in my notice, Brandon, I *am* a waitress. An Angel Club angel. What I do at the university during the day doesn't change the fact. I *am* a waitress, no more or less typical than any of the other waitresses there. That was how you met me, that was how you knew me, that was what attracted you. I *wasn't* the sort of woman you valued."

"But I went ahead and fell in love just the same," he remarked softly.

Audrey nodded. "So did I." Timidly she reached for his hand next to hers on the smooth wooden surface of the table. His knuckles felt warm against her fingers, and she molded them gently to his. "It's not that my research is wrong, Brandon. When I deal with generalities I'm right on target. But you aren't a generality. You don't fit the profile. It was hard for me to acknowledge that, so I tried not to. But I'm enough of a scientist to know that I can't fight the truth, Brandon. I do love you."

He twisted his hand to capture hers, and squeezed it. His thumb ran the length of hers, and he kept his vision fixed on the slender bones of her wrist. "If we're going to be swapping confessions," he said quietly, "then I guess it's my turn."

Her eyes widening, she smiled. "Be my guest," she invited him. "Confess to your heart's content."

He continued to study her fragile hand enfolded in his and grinned sheepishly. "I *am* a little boy with fantasies," he admitted. "You showed me that, and while I'm not a scientist, I know I can't fight the truth either. It doesn't matter that I believe in women's lib, that I want my woman to be my equal, that I try to follow the party line. I still have my little-boy fantasies about women, and knowing you made me accept that fact."

"There's nothing wrong with fantasies."

He looked at her questioningly.

Audrey's smile expanded. "Okay, tell me about your fantasies, and I'll tell you if there's anything wrong with them."

He perused her face, then inhaled. "After I met you, Audrey, that first time at the Angel Club...I lay awake the entire night, fantasizing about you in my bedroom." He lifted his eyes hopefully to hers. "Will you indulge a little boy's fantasies?"

She gazed into his open face, his eyes aglow with yearning, his lips parted beseechingly. He *did* forgive her, she realized with a surge of gratitude. He did accept her for what she was, for what she'd done. All he wanted in return was for her to accept what he was.

She answered his question by leaning forward and pressing her mouth to his. His hand tightened on hers, and he tugged her off the stool to stand between his outstretched legs. His kiss spread fire through her, warmer and more intoxicating than the Irish coffee she'd consumed. When she raised her hands to his head and combed her fingers through his soft blond hair, he moaned and drew in a sharp breath. Standing, he lifted her into his arms.

Without moving his lips from hers, he carried her down the hall and kicked open the door to his bedroom. At the side of the bed he lowered her to her feet. "Let me see you in here," he whispered, backing up a step and absorbing her presence in his room.

She skimmed the room with her eyes, appreciating its clean, masculine decor, the plush easy chair in one corner, the square bureau, and the thick Persian rug beneath her stockinged feet. Turning back to Brandon, she instantly noticed the delight radiating from his eyes. "Do I fulfill the fantasy?" she asked.

A smile teased his lips as he circled her, studying her from different angles. "Your wings are crushed," he observed, touching the wire and mesh protruding from her uniform below her shoulders.

"That's the way it is with reality sometimes," she quipped. "It clips your wings."

"I guess I don't really like this outfit after all," he decided. "Fantasies notwithstanding, it doesn't suit you."

"At least not when I haven't got socks jammed down the front," she mocked herself.

He glided back to her and slid his hands from her waist upward, filling them with the modest swells of her breasts. "Thank God for small blessings," he murmured as he lowered his mouth to her throat.

"Small is right." She laughed hazily, and then her laughter dissolved into a throaty sigh as he reached for the shoulder straps and eased them down her arms. Once she was naked to the waist, his lips traveled downward, closing over one nipple. She sighed again, her fingers reaching for the back of his shirt and freeing it from the waistband of his trousers.

He pulled away from her and straightened up. "I'm liberated enough to want you to undress me," he whispered hoarsely. "If you think you can manage it this time."

She obliged, working down the buttons of his shirt and then shoving it off his wide shoulders. He let it fall to the floor as her hands danced across the rugged muscular breadth of his chest, reveling in the glinting golden curls of hair that tapered down to his lean abdomen.

"Will you have to return the uniform when you quit your job at the Angel Club?" he asked as her fingers attacked the buckles of his belt.

"No," she replied. "I had to buy it when I took the job." When the belt came undone he groaned softly, a passionate sound that unleashed a matching burst of passion within Audrey. "Why do you ask? Deep in your little-boy heart you *do* like it, don't you," she tenderly accused him.

"Not the uniform," he admitted, sliding it past her hips and down her legs. "But the stockings..." He ran his palms over the dark lace covering her thighs, and she savored the friction of the mesh against his skin. "I do like the stockings."

"Hmmm." She pretended disapproval, but her smile gave her away. "Okay, the stockings. But I'm not going to wear those damned shoes for you. They're real backbreakers, Brandon."

"The last thing I'd want is for you to break that beautiful back of yours," he swore, rotating her so he could view the smooth pale skin of her back. He languorously peeled down the stockings, dropping to his knees to slide them off her feet. He rose and tossed them onto his dresser, then turned to face her again.

Somehow she succeeded in unfastening his zipper and removing his trousers. Her hands lingered on his hard hips, and he pulled her snugly against himself. "You know, Audrey, fantasies are a lot like principles," he breathed into her hair.

"In what way?"

"Neither of them can hold a candle to reality." He guided her to the bed and they stretched out together, their legs interwoven and their hands freely exploring each other's bodies. Audrey felt her love and desire for him swelling, filling her, building to a nearly unbearable intensity. She let her hands cover him, but he pushed them away. "Slowly this time," he murmured. "Let me prove what a gentleman I am."

"You've already proved it," she insisted, but he determinedly set his own leisurely pace, pinning her hands to the mattress to prevent her from touching him. His lips roamed from her shoulder down her arm, savoring every inch of skin in their path until he reached her wrist and nipped it with his teeth. She moaned, her hips writhing against him, her thighs locked tensely about one of his.

He shifted, moving his mouth to her hip, journeying upward now in search of her breasts. He suckled first one and then the other, his body rising onto hers. He tasted the hollow of her throat, the underside of her jaw, her chin. "I'm glad you aren't a madonna," he whispered.

"In your little-boy fantasies I'm a whore?" she asked, half-serious.

"No. In my fantasies—my grown-man fantasies—
you're a woman," he stated. "That's all I ever want you
to be."

He released her hands and she let them rediscover the
strong arch of his back as he lifted himself slightly. One of
his hands settled between her legs, caresssing her, stoking
the blazing hunger within her until she emitted a soft sob
of frustration. She moved with him, opening to him, her
entire body aching, needing, demanding. Clearly he sensed
her almost desperate craving, and, gentleman that he was,
he gave himself fully to her, satisfying his own hunger as
he satisfied hers.

She wrapped her legs around him, drawing him deep
into herself. She wanted him to know that she was all he
ever wanted her to be—a woman who could trust him, who
could love him, who could accept the truth of her love even
as it defied her logic, her experience and her intellect. Their
bodies strove together toward that truth, that ultimate,
shattering truth that neither of them was willing or able to
deny any longer. Audrey sensed it looming ahead, just beyond her reach, and she hurtled herself toward it, trusting
Brandon to carry her there, to deliver her to an understanding that transcended everything but the simple truth
of her love for him.

She arrived in a dazzling eruption, a rapturous cascade
of sensation, pulsing in shimmering waves through her.
She felt the tension in his muscles, the fierceness of his
motions as he followed her over the peak and succumbed
to his own ecstasy with a ragged groan. Still she couldn't
let go of him. She wanted him here with her, forever,
burning with her in the devouring fire of truth that ignited them both.

Eventually his breath became more regular, and her
heartbeat slowed to an even tempo. Her arms relaxed

against his waist, and he rolled off her, settling wearily onto the mattress and hugging her close to himself. "Audrey," he sighed. "Audrey..." As if that was all that needed to be said.

Her gaze focused on his face. Sweet exhaustion illuminated his eyes and softened his lips. "Brandon," she whispered, running her index finger over the sleek line of his jaw. "Brandon, it was very nice of you—"

"Nice?" he hooted.

She shook her head. "The last time, Brandon...when you asked me if I was protected. That was nice of you. Men don't usually bother to worry about such things—"

"I'm not a usual man," he reminded her almost indignantly.

"No," she quickly agreed. "You're not. I was wrong to react the way I did then."

"I was wrong to imply what I did," he acknowledged. "But Audrey, if we decide to spend the rest of our lives apologizing for our mistakes with each other, it's going to get pretty boring awfully soon."

"I agree," she said. "So we should get all the apologizing done right now. I'm sorry I overreacted, and I'm sorry I misjudged you, and—"

"It's getting boring already," he playfully silenced her.

She grinned, then leaned toward him and kissed him. "One last apology," she insisted. He rolled his eyes in dismay, but she forged ahead. "I'm sorry I mistook Karen for your girlfriend. That was really stupid of me."

"No, it wasn't," he consoled her. "She's an attractive young woman and there we were, having dinner together on a date. It was an easy situation to misread."

"She's a wonderful friend," Audrey remarked. "Not only for you but for me. When I talked to her this afternoon, Brandon, she told me you loved me, and I was driving you nuts, and if I didn't do something about it right away she'd string me up by my thumbs.''

Brandon closed his eyes and let out a roar of laughter. "She said that?" he groaned. "*She's* the one who deserves to be strung up!''

"Nonsense," Audrey defended Karen. "She was absolutely correct. She's a very candid woman and I like her."

Brandon's laughter subsided, leaving in its wake a dimpled smile. "She's a nosy little busybody, but I suppose you sisters have to stick up for each other."

"She calls you Bran," Audrey commented. "Is that what you like to be called?"

"Not particularly," he admitted. "It makes me sound like a bowl of cereal. But Karen gets a notion in her head and she won't be shaken from it. I've given up telling her not to call me Bran."

"Now I suppose you'll be telling me not to call you Fox."

He considered, then nodded. "You only call me Fox when you're angry with me, I've noticed."

"Then don't make me angry," she warned him.

"I'd much rather make you happy."

"I'd say you've demonstrated a knack for that."

His pleasure at her compliment showed in his smile, in his hand gently cupping over her shoulder, holding her closer. "I'd also like to think I've got a knack for making you honest," he commented quietly. "You're the first woman I've ever met who's managed to make an honest man out of me. I ought to make an honest woman out of you."

"You already have," Audrey pointed out.

"Not legally. I *am* a lawyer, don't forget."

She leaned back, trying to interpret his words. "Is this a proposal?"

Her surprised expression seemed to amuse him. "I already tried propositioning you, and look where that got me," he reminded her. "A proposal is obviously the better route to take with someone like you."

"Are you sure? Are you sure that's really what you want, Brandon?"

His amusement waned as he digested her bewildered look. "I'm sure that you're everything I've ever wanted in a woman—including a few things I didn't even know I wanted."

"Like black lace stockings?"

"Like someone as sexy as she's brilliant, someone as exciting as she's brainy. Someone who's neither a madonna nor a whore, but something incredibly magnificent in between. To say nothing of someone who can teach me a few things at bridge." He sighed, growing solemn. "Audrey, I don't want to rush you—"

"Oh, for heaven's sake, rush me," she demanded. "By all means, rush me! I love you, Brandon. Of course I'll marry you."

He took several moments to register her acceptance, and his smile returned. "But you've got to promise not to try to solve all my litigation the way you did today," he cautioned her. "And you've got to promise to leave me out of your research."

"Oho, so you wait till I say yes before you start laying down the conditions," she teased with pretended annoyance. "Maybe I'd better rethink the whole thing."

"Don't you dare," he warned her before pressing her onto her back and silencing her with a kiss.

Her arms closed imperatively around him, and she knew that she didn't have to rethink anything. Brandon had made her recognize the truth, and that was something she didn't have to think about or research. And as her soul strengthened in the passionate love he had awakened in her, she accepted, exulted, and surrendered to joy.

Silhouette Desire

MARCH TITLES

GOLDEN GODDESS
Stephanie James

RIVER OF DREAMS
Naomi Horton

TO HAVE IT ALL
Robin Elliot

LEADER OF THE PACK
Diana Stuart

FALSE IMPRESSIONS
Ariel Berk

WINTER MEETING
Doreen Owens Malek